Snowbound Hearts

MINA BECKETT

CURTISSLYNN
PUBLISHING

Other Books by Mina Beckett

Coldiron Cowboys series

The Heartbreak Cowboy (includes the prequel novella, _The Cowboy's Goodnight Kiss_)

The Fallen Cowboy

Breaking the Cowboy

Coldiron Cowboys Collection - includes all three books plus, the novella.

Crossfire Canyon series

A Cold Montana Christmas: A Crossfire Canyon Novel

Rough Creek series

A Cowboy Charming Christmas

Hollywood Cowboy

Dangerous Desires series

Secrets Behind the Masquerade

Cowboy Temptation series

Trapped In Temptation

Coming soon: Texas Heat Series

Roughneck Cowboy

For more information about books, excerpts, contests, cover reveal, and release dates visit _www.minabeckett.com_

Or join my _Romantic Reader_ newsletter.

Introduction

Dear Reader,

Snowbound Hearts is a story born from the pages of <u>Hollywood Cowboy</u>, part of my Rough Creek series. The hero, Morgan Prescott, a sexy cowboy, heartthrob actor, finds himself auditioning for a role in a film adaptation of *Snowbound Hearts*, written by none other than Blane Seward, fictional bestselling author extraordinaire. So, while this novel stands on its own, I hope those who have read Hollywood Cowboy will be delighted to see the storyline come to life.

Chapter One

THERE WERE NO CERTAINTIES IN LIFE OTHER than death. No promises constructed by a grand designer.

No scheme.

No plan.

There was only the here and now. That's what Tamara had always said.

Sweet, sweet Tamara.

The plane of existence where Dwight Murtagh, his wife Tamara, and his son, Liam, had once lived in harmony was now a distant memory.

Lost to the past.

An indistinct dimension of time in which one's life persisted only in the vague and fading recollections of bittersweet moments, forever etched into the vastness of the ages.

The past held no structure, no form. No life. It was simply a torturous reminder of all he'd lost to death's unyielding grip. It floated in and out of Dwight's mind in the murky twilight of sleep, enveloping his heart with its icy tendrils and squeezing sometimes so hard he thought he might die.

But he hadn't. Not yet.

Like a carefully choreographed performance on a staged set, life, with all its senses and emotions, continued to unfold. Second by second, time would shift from that dreadful here and now, to gone.

A hard blast of Arctic wind barreled into Dwight's midsection, causing him to hunch over and seek refuge deeper within his sheep-skin coat. He trembled slightly, pulling firmly on the reins of his buckskin steed, Bane, steering him, along with the pack mule, Moose, back towards the safety of home. His intended three-day trip to the supply cabin at the cattle station had been abruptly shortened by the rapidly darkening skies and the imminent storm.

Over the past hour, the whimsical snow flurries of the afternoon were steadily increasing. Soon they'd transform into a tempest of snow and eventually, ice. The powerful storm front that national weather channels and local meteorologists had been warning the inhabitants of Copper Creek about had launched its relentless crawl across the expanse of the Rocky Mountains and now descended upon Dwight's tiny corner of the world. The Sweet Surrender Ranch.

The name was a bitter irony, for surrender was a luxury Dwight could no longer afford. He'd had to forge ahead, not just for himself, but for Liam. Despite the boy's tender age of six, they'd learned to navigate the uncertain landscape of life, seeking solace in each other's company as they confronted the emptiness left behind by Tamara's passing.

It's been two years, Dwight, her gentle, guiding voice reminded him.

"Two long years, honey."

Let me go.

Grief constricted his chest with such force that he

thought his heart might cease to pump. He couldn't. Not now. Not ever. "I can't," he whispered.

The bitter wind snatched his tears and transformed them to ice. They clung there beneath his eyes, frozen, brittle crystals glinting in the faint light of the setting sun. His heart felt just as frozen, numb and heavy in his chest.

It was still fragile, as though one wrong move could make it fracture. He guarded himself against the memories that now felt sharp as shattered glass. Even a small reminder of happier times could pierce through his defenses and break what remained of his spirit into countless shards of pain. His tears, though seldom and always released in private, were a physical reminder of the anguish now solidified within him.

As the wind howled and snow swirled around him, Dwight steeled himself for the ride back to the ranch. The storm was just another obstacle to overcome, a reminder that even in the darkest moments, he had to find a way to carry on.

For in the absence of certainties and grand designs, the love he had for Liam was the one thing that remained steadfast. He lived and breathed for his son, and he would keep the promise he'd made to his wife all those years ago.

He would do everything in his power to see that Liam was raised right, that he had a strong moral foundation to stand on and that he would know how much his mother and father loved him.

Dwight felt like a hollow shell on the inside, but as long as he drew breath, he would continue to honor the memory of his sweet Tamara and cherish the short life they had built together here on this vast spread of Montana land.

As the sun's final ray dipped behind the mountain,

casting the landscape into shadow, Dwight hoisted his drooping shoulders, wiped his face, and steered the horses towards home.

He hadn't traveled more than a few paces when something in the distance caught his eye. A small, yet brilliant beam of light pierced the purple veil of snow and twilight.

It was a vehicle. The rumble of the struggling engine echoed like an explosion in Dwight's quiet world.

A single thought crossed his mind: who was foolish enough to be traveling in such weather? This afternoon, the tight-knit crew of cowhands he had employed at the ranch had secured the livestock within the safety of the barns. Now, they were nestled warmly in the bunkhouse, settled around a crackling fire, playing cards to pass the time, as the storm unleashed its fury outside. The residence of Copper Creek, well-acquainted with the harshness of winter weather, knew better than to venture out with a storm warning in effect.

Navigating the Montana backcountry presented a formidable challenge, even to those well-versed in its rugged terrain. The vast expanse of wilderness was a labyrinth of remote canyons, jagged peaks, and dense forests that seemed to stretch on for eternity. In some areas, the so-called roads were little more than dirt trails, carved into the landscape by the passage of time and the hooves of wild animals.

Trails, often hidden beneath a blanket of snow or overgrown foliage, demanded exceptional skill and intuition to traverse. It was not uncommon for inexperienced travelers to find themselves disoriented; their sense of direction confounded by the deceptive beauty of the wild. As the vehicle drew closer, Dwight narrowed his eyes against the snowstorm, attempting to recognize its distinctive features. It was a late-model Ford truck, bathed in a shade of blue.

No one he knew.

The truck tires cut a swath over the lacy blanket of white covering the ground, leaving behind a wake of dark ruts that clung to the dirt road long after they had passed.

The only nearby ranch was the Brewster place. Ronnie Brewster had passed away over a year ago without any family, as far as Dwight knew. Perhaps the property had been sold.

The ranch house had been decrepit even when Ronnie was alive. If the driver of the truck had sought shelter there, they would have found nothing but a dilapidated shell, offering barely more protection than the howling blizzard outside.

Why would anyone risk traveling in such treacherous conditions? After all, no one would risk driving this far into the wilderness unless they were lost, desperate, or downright mad.

But what if...

Dread coiled in Dwight's stomach, hard and unyielding. The last time a vehicle had arrived at the ranch under such circumstances, it brought the devastating news of his wife's untimely passing. A wave of renewed sorrow washed over him. He couldn't bear to go through that again. He couldn't take the news that someone else he loved was dead. But with Liam safely back at the ranch, he was less worried about this being another harbinger of bad news.

It was simply someone lost in the storm, and he knew he couldn't ignore them. The storm was dangerous. Another thought stuck in his gut. If the occupants of the truck didn't turn around, he'd be entertaining strangers for a week or until the snow melted.

He cursed under his breath, knowing he had to intercept that rust bucket.

Dwight loathed talking to people, more so now that he was practically a recluse. But something other than the daunting task of politeness scratched at his brain.

As he turned Bane towards the road, he couldn't shake the uneasy feeling that crept into his gut, the sensation that this unexpected visitor might bring with them a change that would irrevocably alter the course of his life.

Through the curtain of white, he saw the truck fishtail. The driver's attempts to slow down were futile - the brakes locked, and the rubber simply glided on top of snow. The truck only gained speed as it raced downhill. He knew it would never make the turn to avoid going into the creek at the bottom of the hill.

"Yah!" he yelled, spurring the horses to run.

He prayed he was wrong and that by some miracle, the truck would find traction and plow safely into one of the snow drifts alongside the road. But an instant later, the driver overcorrected. The vehicle spun around and veered straight towards the creek.

"Help me!" came the distant cry of a female voice from inside the truck cab as it hinged on the edge.

"God, no," he whispered.

You have to help her, Dwight.

"I know, honey," he answered, feeling his heart quicken. "I know."

The horses galloped over the bridge, their hooves thundering in a rapid staccato as they climbed the opposite bank of the stream. Dwight jumped off his horse and rushed to the vehicle's driver side.

The woman's wide, almond-shaped brown eyes were filled with terror and desperation as she pressed her palms against the cold, glass window. A large, deep purple bruise adorned her right cheek, blemishing her otherwise pale complexion. Her trembling voice was a desperate plea for help, raw with fear and vulnerability. "Please! Help us!" she cried out.

Dwight's focus shifted to the gray bearded man in the passenger seat, his body slumped and lifeless against the door. A deep gash on his side oozed thick crimson blood, staining the fabric of his shirt and the leather seat. Fear and urgency clawed at Dwight as he took in the sight, his mind racing with thoughts of how to help the injured man. Gripping the door handle, he gave it a hard yank, but it wouldn't budge.

"Roll the window down!" he ordered.

Her nod was a frantic, up and down movement. The window was stubborn, lowering only a fraction with each crank.

"Roll faster!" he yelled.

"I'm trying!"

Dwight heard something under the truck give way. It shifted and the woman froze.

If he didn't act fast, he was going to lose them both.

"No." Cold chills blanketed his body as his mind went to Tamara. If only he'd been there to help her. "Cover your face," he ordered, swearing he wouldn't let this woman die.

She flinched and turned her head away as he lifted his elbow, preparing to shatter the window. But in a sudden, violent motion, the front of the truck jolted forward, lifting the back end into the air like a sinking ship. The metal body let out an ominous groan and the front of the truck plunged nose first over the edge of the bank.

Driven by instinct, Dwight's hand shot out to seize the handle once more, a desperate, final attempt to prevent the truck from skidding into the creek. But his exertions proved futile against the imposing mass of the vehicle.

Despite his desperate grip, the truck continued its slide, an inexorable descent towards the edge of the creek. The gravel beneath the tires crunched and shifted, offering no purchase against the vehicle's weight. With a stomach-churning lurch, the truck teetered on the precipice before plunging over the edge.

A gasp tore from his throat as the world tilted and his fingers slipped from the handle. He watched helplessly as the truck continued to slide in what seemed like slow motion, headed straight for the creek.

He held his breath as the inevitable collision loomed. The sickening sound of twisting metal and shattering glass filled the air as the truck hit the bank and bounced into the frigid water below.

Dwight stood at the edge of the creek, his breath heaving, his heart hammering. The metallic tang of adrenaline filled his mouth, but the surreal nature of the event still clung to him. He couldn't shake the feeling of being trapped within a nightmare. Yet, the cold reality of the sinking truck was a stark counterpoint to his disbelief. The dreamlike fog began to clear, replaced by the harsh clarity of the situation. He wasn't asleep. This was terrifyingly real.

The shrill of the woman's terrified voice rang out, echoing in the snowy air.

He launched into action. He yanked the rope from his saddle, securing it onto the horn with practiced ease. Then he retrieved the small flashlight from the pocket of his coat, tossed the garment onto a rock. He placed the flashlight between his teeth, its metallic taste cold against his tongue.

He secured his grip on the rope and started over the

edge, knowing Bane would keep resistance and not move from the edge until he gave the order.

The flashlight's beam bobbed in rhythm with his movements as he propelled down, casting an eerie glow on the icy bank as he used the rope to navigate the treacherous terrain.

He paused near the water to assess the surroundings and strategize his next move. The position of the truck made him fear the worse if it was swept away by the fast-moving current. Water poured into the cab through the busted windshield.

"Help!"

"I'm coming!"

Somewhere amid the chaos and panic, night had fallen. The relentless snowfall stung every inch of his exposed skin, while the wind howled and buffeted him from all angles. The blistering cold was already intense, but it was nothing compared to the biting sensation of wading into the water up to his knees. Even with his well-insulated boots and lined Wrangler jeans, he couldn't escape the penetrating chill that seeped through his bones.

"Oh! God!" she screamed and began beating against the back glass. "Hurry! It's filling with water!"

He anchored his boot on the bumper, climbed over the tailgate, and sprinted to the window. "Get back!"

"Please!" she begged. "I don't want to die!"

"Cover your face."

She obeyed, covering her head and turning away. He hammered the window with his flashlight until it splintered, then kicked it in and reached for her.

She clung to his hands, and he yanked her free of the cab, landing on his back in a surge of adrenaline and relief.

Easy. She could have injuries.

"No," he reassured Tamara. "I don't think any-thing's broken."

The woman, miraculously devoid of severe injuries from the crash, trembled in Dwight's arms. She clung to him, and he let himself pretend she was the voice inside his head, the missing part of his heart –is beloved wife. "Oh, my sweet Tamara. I've got you. You're safe, honey. You're safe."

But the tender moment was a fleeting one as the man trapped inside the truck cab began to moan.

The woman clutched Dwight's shirt, snapping him back to their dangerous reality. "You've got to help Hogue! Please! He's hurt!"

Saving one life from the icy clutch of the creek was challenging enough, saving two seemed an insurmount-able task.

Dwight once again examined the precarious scene. The truck's rear end teetered on the brink of the creek, a seemingly minor shift in water away from a plunge into the lethal depths. Any sudden movement, and the op-portunity to make it safely to the shore would be lost to the merciless current.

Since Tamara's untimely departure, Dwight had often pondered over the final moments of his existence. He'd imagined that when the end drew near, he'd wel-come it with a sense of resignation, perhaps even relief.

However, now, as he stood on the precipice of mor-tality, feeling the cold specter of death inching closer, it didn't seem as inviting as he had envisaged. The com-forting shroud of acceptance he'd imagined was starkly absent. Instead, there was a raw edge to his fear, a primal instinct to survive that he hadn't expected.

This instinct, this will to live surged through his veins, countering the encroaching cold, revitalizing his numb extremities, and imbuing him with a strength he didn't know he had. The sensation was as startling as it was terrifying. He was not ready to give in, not ready to let go. His fight to rescue them and himself had only just begun.

He steadied the woman. "Can you make it to the bank without me?" Her nod, though jerky, was affirmative. "Then go and don't look back no matter what happens." With trembling limbs, she crawled over the tailgate and waded into the creek.

Dwight turned his attention back to the cab, now brimming with water. "Hogue!" he yelled, hoping to stir the man into consciousness. Droplets of ice had formed on the tips of his gray beard. His face was ashen, and his thin body was motionless. Was he even breathing?

Reaching in, Dwight placed his hands under Hogue's armpits, pulled him up and over the back of the seat and through the shattered window. Though the man was thin, maneuvering him over the tailgate, over his shoulder and through the icy water was a staggering task.

He deposited Hogue on the snow-covered bank and turned his gaze towards the woman.

The numbing cold had rendered him insensate to the water's icy bite, but its forceful current was a formidable opponent, making each step a struggle. Eventually, he reached the bank, gently laying Hogue on the rocky ground.

"Is he breathing?" the woman's voice was a desperate whisper, her hands clutching at Hogue's flannel shirt. "Please don't die!" Her plea cut through the howling wind of the storm and rushing current of the water.

Dwight knew it was going to take more than begging to save the man's life. But a surge of empathy gripped his heart, the stark terror in her eyes serving as a haunting reflection of his own anguish. The void carved by Tamara's unexpected death was still a raw, pulsating wound within him, one that he was certain would never fully mend. The pain was a relentless undercurrent in his life, a reminder of the love lost and the healing that seemed forever out of reach.

He had to push through those feelings if he were going to get them out of this. Taking the woman by the arm, Dwight brought her to her feet. "Listen to me," he shouted over the roar of the rushing water. He knew he couldn't carry them both, but with her help, they all might have a chance. "The rope is tied to my horse at the top. He'll do the work. All you have to do is hold on. Can you do that for me— for Hogue?"

His gaze locked onto hers, seeking confirmation. With a nod from her, he felt a flicker of hope.

Chapter Two

Dwight tied the rope around her waist, carefully positioned her in front of him, and guided her hands onto the rope. Subsequently, he tied the rope around his own waist, ensuring it was secure, and hoisted Hogue onto his shoulder with a firm grip and shoved the flashlight into his back pocket. They were making the climb in the dark and with winds strong enough to topple trees.

"Ready?" he asked, taking the rope with his free hand.

"Yes!" came Anna's resolute response, her hands tightly gripping the rope.

Dwight blew the command whistle, the unique sound he had trained Bane to respond to, and immediately felt the rope tighten. The rope began to move, and they began their cautious climb up the embankment, each step taken with deliberate care.

Ascent up the snow-covered hillside was backbreaking. Dwight had to bear the weight of Hogue on his shoulders and prayed the woman was strong enough to keep a hold of the rope. Each step was difficult, an exhausting battle against the icy chill and perilous potential hazards. They continued to inch upwards, slowly but surely making their way towards safety. Bane maintained tension on the rope that was their lifeline.

He watched as she climbed up the steep incline, her fancy black boots with a heel trying to bite into the rocky terrain. Her feet slipped beneath a white blanket of powdery flakes more than once, but she never gave up.

He admired her tenacity but would have gladly traded it for a decent pair of hiking boots with treads.

Finally, they reached the top. She collapsed on the ground. "Thank you, God," she whispered over and over in panting breaths that echoed into the night.

Dwight laid Hogue on the ground and fell to his knees beside her, his breath misting in the icy air. He was physically fit and used to strenuous activity, but it was a tough climb for him as well. Exhausted but triumphant, he aimed the flashlight down at the creek, the truck now fully submerged.

He'd done it.

Against all odds, he had saved two lives from the icy grasp of death. But with the storm raging, the fight for survival, it seemed, was far from over.

The woman moved to Hogue. "He's alive, isn't he?"

"Barely," he answered.

This was the first instance when Dwight truly took in her appearance. She wasn't dressed for a blizzard.

Her attire was alarmingly ill-suited for the harsh weather conditions they found themselves in. She wasn't simply unprepared - she was wholly unequipped for even the slightest hint of snow.

Hell, she wasn't dressed for Montana in February.

Period.

Drenched from head to toe, her clothes were growing stiff and crunchy from the ice that had formed on them. The frigid water clung to her skin like a second layer, soaking through the thin, pale blue blouse she wore. Her designer jeans, decorated with deliberate distress and strategically placed rips, did little to insulate her from the frigid temperatures. But it was her changing color that had Dwight concerned. With each gust of wind, her exposed skin turned a bright shade of red, an alarming contrast to her creamy complexion before the truck entered the water.

Dwight was scratching his head at the contradiction before him. She had a tenacious spirit and a lot of grit. But her careless attitude towards the untamed wilderness was damn foolish.

Through tears and chattering teeth, she looked up at him. "Thank you."

The frosty air had soaked her hair, turning it into a tangled mess that clung to her face like a shroud. Each strand was adorned with glistening snowflakes, giving her the appearance of an icy angel. She couldn't have been more than twenty-five, or any younger than eighteen – an age both too young and too old for the tragedy that could have befallen her and might still yet if Hogue didn't make it.

But he had to give her hope or at least let her hang onto what she had. The cold, crisp air lacked taste, yet it left a numbing sensation on his tongue, as if freezing the words, he might say.

"Thank me when we're all safe and dry," he said untying the rope from around his waist as she stood. He helped her to her feet then quickly freed her from the rope, knowing if they didn't get to the ranch soon, hypothermia would be a major issue.

Dwight retrieved his coat from where he'd thrown it earlier, gave it a shake to remove the snow and slid it on. His muscles protested even the slightest movement. Every fiber of his being screamed in a kind of numbness that brought with it a unique pain. The bone-chilling creek water had infiltrated his clothes, now frozen stiff around him like an unwelcome second skin.

His toes felt as if they were encased in ice, and much like his tongue, buzzed with the sensation of cold-induced numbness. His hands, though sheathed in gloves, failed to fend off the frosty tendrils of the biting chill.

Each reach and step felt as if he was breaking through ice. It seemed as though the chill was penetrating his very bones, a deep cold that no amount of shivering could dispel. His body trembled involuntarily, a futile rebuttal to the ruthless winter cold that he knew wasn't ending anytime soon.

The storm was relentless, whipping tiny ice daggers against his exposed skin. His breath came out in ragged puffs, each exhale forming a ghostly cloud in the frigid air. The once familiar sensation of warmth was but a distant memory, replaced now by the numbing cold that gnawed relentlessly at his fingers and toes.

The wind cut through it like a knife, each gust sending a fresh blast of arctic air over him. His teeth chattered uncontrollably. His breath was ragged. His lungs burned.

Despite the overwhelming desire to succumb to the cold, to just close his eyes and let the snow swallow him whole, Dwight pressed on. Each step was an exercise in sheer willpower, a defiance against the forces of nature. But he knew he had to keep moving. Liam was waiting for him, depending on him. And he would not let the cold defeat him.

Extracting a blanket from the saddle bag, he approached the woman. Her small frame was hunched over Hogue, her body trembling from the biting cold.

With a gentleness that contradicted his frustration, Dwight draped the blanket over her shoulders. It swallowed her small form, offering a meager barrier against the unyielding winter that surrounded them. As the rough fabric settled around her, he noticed her shivers subside slightly, a small victory against the brutal cold.

She shrugged off the blanket with a swift motion, laying it over Hogue as if it were the most natural thing in the world, then glanced at Dwight. Sensing he might disapprove, she explained. "I'm stronger than he is."

Even though he wasn't too thrilled about her decision, there was no denying her determination. Dwight might've been miffed at her for tossing the blanket, but he couldn't help but respect her gumption. She wasn't just talking about physical strength. There was a fire in her spirit that the biting cold couldn't touch. And truth be told, he didn't doubt her strength for a second.

But he kept his thoughts unvoiced after noticing the subtle shift in her posture. It was as if she was bracing herself for a physical blow.

Oh, Dwight, Tamara's soft voice cut in. *Someone's hurt her.*

He gritted his teeth, trying to dismiss his wife's ethereal intuition, and averted his gaze from the woman, shining the flashlight into the blinding white expanse. He could deal with the wreck, the icy water, the bitter cold and the threat of losing all ten of his toes to frostbite. But the thought of someone causing harm to the small, half-frozen woman attending to Hogue was something he found unbearable. He just couldn't, so he shoved that thought aside and concentrated on the problem. Getting them to safety.

He rummaged through his gear, pulling out a second blanket. He unfolded it with a swift shake and once again, draped it over her shoulders. "I didn't go through all the trouble of saving you just to let you become a human popsicle."

With her frost-nipped fingers, she clutched the edges of the blanket, pulling it over her head and wrapping it tightly around her trembling body.

"What's your name?"

"Anna."

That's a pretty name.

He supposed it was, though now didn't seem like the best time to mull over the beauty of one's name. "I'm Dwight Murtaugh," he stated factually and kept his eyes on lookout for the pack horse. He knew that despite the raging blizzard, Moose would remember his training and remain nearby.

When the light caught a black mane, Dwight pulled his lips inward and released a shrill whistle. The horse's ears perked, and he slowly emerged from beneath a cover of a large cedar and trotted towards him.

He shined the flashlight at Anna, and she squinted as the harsh beam reached her eyes. "There's shelter, a warm fire and food back at my place."

"Your place?" she echoed, unsteadily rising to her feet.

"That's right," he answered, his eyes catching the wave of fear that abruptly washed over her features.

She's at the mercy of a stranger. A rather large and grumpy stranger. Of course, she's apprehensive about going home with you.

"I'm not grumpy," he mumbled, knowing Tamara was right. She always was, but right now... he sighed and restated his Stetson.

It was damn hard to be kind to stupidity. Tonight, Anna had risked all their lives by being foolish. She'd driven into the back end of God's country in the middle of a blizzard. She had to have known there was a risk something like this would happen.

She's running...

We don't know that.

Look at her.

I'd rather not.

Because you know I'm right.

Dwight grabbed Moose's bridle and moved him in place behind Bane. "I'm all you have, lady. You and the old man can stay here and freeze to death or take your chances with me. It's your choice."

Some choice.

Considering her options, Anna swallowed, looked down at Hogue, then squared her shoulders and brought her attention back to Dwight. "I'll do whatever you want. Just save him."

A chill of a different kind crept up Dwight's backbone. All he wanted was to assure her that he meant her no harm, that he'd never ask such a thing of a woman — sexual favors for safety and warmth — but he couldn't muster the words.

Clenching his jaw, he walked to Moose and with brisk efficiency, he unloaded the supplies and equipment from the horse. Taking an emergency blanket from one of the packs, he placed it around Anna's shoulders. "Don't wander off."

Knowing the man was wounded, he carefully lifted Hogue into his arms then, positioned him over the saddle, securing him in place with a sturdy rope. It was a task he'd performed before; just last year, he'd had to secure Bruce Welch in a similar manner after the man succumbed to a heart attack at the cow camp during the spring roundup. As he tightened the rope, Dwight hoped that for Anna's sake, this man wouldn't meet the same grim end.

"Get on," he instructed her using the same biting tone as when he'd told her to stay put.

"Yeah, um, okay," she said, teeth chattering as her

eyes cautiously studied Bane's saddle. It was clear she'd never attempted to mount a horse before.

Of course, she hasn't.

Be nice.

Dwight wasn't sure he remembered how.

"Grab hold of the—" Without warning, a powerful gust of wind slammed into her cold and exhausted frame, nearly sweeping her off her feet. Flinching from the bite, but refusing to go down, she caught hold of the reins. Weaving on her feet, she gripped the pommel then, tried lifting her foot to the stirrup but failed. She was simply too weak to get herself onto the saddle.

"I can do it," she assured him in a somewhat panicky voice as if their lives depended on it.

With a growling sound of irritation, Dwight removed the reins from her hands, took hold of her waist and with little effort, hoisted her up and into the saddle's worn leather seat.

Her small hands, red from the freezing water and wind, clutched the horn as he swung his leg over and mounted the horse behind her. "Home," he said, setting their course with one word.

Happy now? he asked his wife.

Immensely, she answered, and he could see her smug expression in his mind's eye.

Aware that Anna lacked the strength to battle the relentless wind, let alone maintain her balance in the saddle, Dwight instinctively looped his arm around her waist like he would have Liam. He pulled her close, anchoring her securely against the sturdy shield of his body.

ANNA HAD NEVER BEEN SO cold or so confused. Her mind was muddled, in a fog of exhaustion and she guessed, the beginning stages of hypothermia.

She didn't want to die, not when the promise of safety was almost within her grasp. She'd escaped Malachi's wrath. She would not die in a snowstorm.

She tucked her chin under the blanket and concentrated on the Brewster Ranch. Hogue had painted such vivid pictures of his childhood home that she could almost see it, even in the blinding snowstorm. She could almost smell the warm, comforting scent of a crackling fireplace and homemade stew on the stove, hear the welcoming creak of the front porch as they would step onto it, feel the comforting solidity of the old wooden walls that promised protection.

She imagined them there, safe and sound. In that place, hidden deep within Copper Creek, Malachi wouldn't find them. The thought was a soothing balm to her tattered nerves. She clung to the belief that everything would be alright, that this nightmare would soon be a distant memory.

But that belief was thin, as thin as the second blanket Dwight had draped over her. Her thoughts, already scattered by the relentless cold, kept drifting back to one painful reality. John was gone. That loss was a gaping void, threatening to swallow her whole.

John's face flashed in her mind, a ghostly image in the middle of the surrounding blackness. His loss was a searing pain, a constant reminder of the justice he was owed.

Anna swore she would not rest until Malachi Wolfe was behind bars. And giving up now, dying in this frozen wilderness, was not an option. It would mean letting John's murderer walk free, and that was something she could not, would not, allow.

She was determined to fight, to survive because without her, the world would never know the truth. The cold could bite, the wind could howl, the snow could blind her, but she would not be stopped. Not until she had fulfilled her promise to John.

Every bone in her body felt as though it had turned to jelly, offering no stability no matter how minuscule her attempted movements were. Her clothes clung to her, icy and rigid, like the frozen strands of her hair. A pervasive sense of weakness had seeped into her, a silent invader leaving her desperately bereft of strength.

As the horse lurched forward, descending a steep incline, Dwight's arms tightened around her. It was this man who had delivered her and Hogue from the jaws of death, who had pulled them back from the precipice of the inevitable end.

A month ago, her rational deduction would have been that he bore no ill intentions towards them. After all, why would someone with a murderous agenda rescue them from the icy grip of death?

The answer lay etched into her soul. Malachi had shifted her perspective, soundly and quickly. She now understood the existence of malevolence in the world, that there were individuals whose evil knew no bounds. Even more chilling was the realization that there were fates far more horrifying than death itself.

Despite the intensity in Dwight's voice when he yelled at her to move away from the glass, his eyes radiated a warmth and compassion that was impossible to fake. His hands, while swift and precise as they checked her for fractures, moved with an unheard of gentleness, stirring a sensation of tenderness she had never experienced before.

Her heart, worn and weary, swelled with renewed hope. Her instincts had been right. There were indeed good people in this world, and Dwight, with his kind eyes and gentle touch, was undoubtedly one of them.

Clutching that thought like she had the rope, Anna nestled her head against the comforting solidity of his chest. As her eyelids gently closed, surrendering to the pull of rest, the steady cadence of his heartbeat reverberated against her ear – a comforting concerto that promised warmth and safety.

Chapter Three

Dwight had dressed sensibly in layers to protect against the cold — thermal underwear under his insulated jeans, wool socks, a thick flannel shirt, and a parka under his heavy coat. But even all those layers couldn't completely defend against the brutal cold inching its way deeper into his skin. He knew his core body temperature was dropping.

He knew he had to hold on, to cling to consciousness for Liam's sake. The boy had already suffered the loss of his mother. He wouldn't make his son an orphan. Liam wasn't going to be left alone in this world. Not on this frigid night, not as long as Dwight still had life in him.

Then there was this waif-like woman in his arms, small, cold and completely relying on him to navigate them through the blinding snowstorm and back to the safety of the ranch.

If he passed out or slipped off the horse, Anna would have no chance of finding her way on her own. Her life and Hogue's depended on him staying alert and Bane's sense of direction, guiding them home.

Gritting his teeth against the cold, Dwight tightened his numb fingers around the reins. He urged the horse onward, squinting ahead for any glimpse of the ranch through the swirling snow.

Before long, the snow turned into tiny pellets of ice, bouncing off of rocks and evergreen branches before coating the ground with a slick layer. It was only a matter of time before the ranch's electricity would go out and the backup generators would kick in.

He adjusted his Stetson to a more stable position on his head and pulled up the collar of his jacket to protect his neck from the biting sting of the elements.

Every second seemed like an eternity as he peered into the blustering whiteout, barely able to see more than a few yards ahead. Then, seemingly out of nowhere, faint lights appeared. The multicolored Christmas lights from the ranch house roof began twinkling through the blizzard. Light's that he'd put up at Liam's request so his mother could see them from heaven.

It'd been a heartbreaking request for Dwight and Lael, his mother-in-law, but he'd done it because a little piece of him hoped his son was right. That Tamara was looking down on them.

And if she was?

What would his wife think of him, her husband, a man who'd vowed to love her and only her, holding another woman in his arms?

A wave of guilt surged within him, causing a bitter taste to rise in his throat.

Though the proximity of his and Anna's bodies was due to a life and death rescue, he'd never felt more uneasy about human contact. She was silent and still in his arms, hardly noticeable. Yet, he couldn't disregard the instinctive response of his body to the appeal of her soft feminine curves. He hadn't been this close to a woman in years. Conflicting sensations ran over him. Longing, comfort and ultimately a sense of betrayal.

Don't feel that way. You're a man. She's a woman.

A married man.

I'm gone, Dwight.

Through Tamara's persuasive words, his mind steadily grew more resolved, urging him to accept what his heart had thus far refused to.

His wife was dead.

He took a deep breath and focused on getting them back to the warmth and safety of the ranch house. As the structure came into view, a sense of relief flooded him—it was one of the most comforting things he'd ever seen.

The winds escalated into a formidable force, causing him to spur his horse into a swift gallop. With Hogue's limp body secured on his back, Moose followed Bane's lead.

The once benign environment of just an hour ago, now roared with an unrestrained tempest, each gust whipping up snow and ice into a blinding, white vortex. The surrounding landscape of barns and fenced-in pastures had morphed into a frenzied spectacle of nature's fury. Under the relentless onslaught of the storm, everything was consumed in a swirling, frenzied dance of white, reducing visibility to a mere sliver of what it once was.

Dwight guided Bane to the back porch and dismounted, holding on tightly to Anna's arm so she wouldn't fall. Her body lay inert, potentially numbed by the shock of the traumatic tumble down the bank, the icy sting of the cold water, and the exhausting climb. Above all, the near-death encounter had seemingly drained the vitality from her, leaving her in a state of torpor.

He slipped her from the horse and secured her in his arms.

His jeans, nearly frozen solid, cracked as he staggered up the steps and into the house.

"Lael!" he called out, desperate to get Anna warm and looked after. Careful not to jostle her too much, he laid her on the couch. "Lael!" he called again. "Are you here?"

She didn't answer.

With a swift pivot, he dashed outside into the storm. He hastily freed Hogue from Moose and with a firm but careful grip, hoisted the man's unconscious form over his shoulder. Commanding the horses towards the barn, he knew they'd weather the storm until he could return to care for them.

After depositing Hogue in the guest bedroom, he went to the message board hanging on the refrigerator and read Lael's handwritten note. "Supper is in the oven. See you at breakfast."

Dwight was thankful Lael had stayed at the ranch to help with Liam after Tamara's accident. It wasn't unusual for Liam to spend the night with his grandma, but tonight of all nights...

Anna required the nurturing presence of a woman, not a grumpy, grieving rancher who had lost his ability to crack a smile and Hogue needed medical attention.

He knew he could call Lael, explain the situation and she'd come running. It was a short walk from the ranch house to the little cabin she called home. But he didn't want her or Liam wandering around in a blizzard.

He reached for the house phone. Pressing the button to dial the bunkhouse, the call connected almost instantly. "Fire up the side-by-side," he commanded.

"Why?" Sonny's voice floated through the line, threaded with a clear note of alarm. "What's wrong?"

"Bring Lael and Liam back to the house. Tell her there's been an accident. I have a man injured and a woman in shock," he relayed.

"On my way," Sonny responded, dispensing with formalities and hanging up without a goodbye.

Dwight ran a palm over his wet beard, another fleeting wave of relief washing over him again. Lael, with her background as a retired E.R nurse, was more than capable. She would be able to manage Hogue's injuries with professional efficiency and as for Anna...

Dwight raked off his Stetson and tossed it into the recliner. He was well-versed in the rudiments of medical care, a skillset honed through handling a multitude of basic first aid situations that punctuated life on the ranch. He could adeptly manage the commonplace cuts, scrapes, burns, and dehydration, and even the less frequent broken bones didn't faze him. As a fourth-generation Montana rancher, he had inherited a wealth of practical knowledge, including the crucial ability to treat hypothermia. The unforgiving Montana winters had taught him the importance of this skill, and the lives it could potentially save, making it an indispensable part of his repertoire.

Yet, he was wasting precious time because the person whom he rescued, and lay half frozen on his couch was a woman. A female who had evoked urges in him he refused to acknowledge.

So lost in his thoughts that he hadn't remembered to remove his jacket, tiny droplets of melted ice and water had begun to form on its surface. They combined and trickled down, soaking the rug beneath him.

Dwight's gaze fell to his boots, caked with a mixture of snow, dirt, and grit picked up from the rescue. Tamara would have been beside herself if she could see him now, his boots leaving a trail of dirty, melting snow on her treasured rugs.

He'd driven her all the way to Idaho to find those rugs, hand-woven masterpieces crafted by Native American artisans. She'd told him that their intricate patterns told stories of the earth, of the sky, of life and tradition.

They were simply rugs to him. But Tamara had fallen in love with the vibrant colors and the rich textures and seeing her so happy had made the price and the long drive worth it.

Dwight couldn't suppress a smile as he remembered the drive back. It had been a beautiful summer weekend; the last summer they'd spent together. The truck's windows had been down, inviting the warm breeze to whip through the cab. Tamara had sat in the passenger seat, her red hair dancing in the wind, her face lit up with joy and satisfaction.

He could still see her there, her cheeks flushed from the summer sun, eyes sparkling with delight as she touched the edges of her newly acquired rugs. They had explored the scenic backroads, stopping at little roadside stalls, diving into local eateries, just enjoying each other's company. Those were the times he cherished, the memories that warmed him now.

But damn it, he'd gone and dirtied the rugs. Her rugs. "Ah, God, honey," he whispered. "I'm sorry."

A wave of irritation and guilt washed over him. It was such a simple thing, removing boots at the door, a basic courtesy that he'd neglected in his rush. He grimaced at the thoughtless mistake. Those boots, so practical and necessary for the harshness of ranch life, had no place on the delicate woven stories of Tamara's rugs.

Snap out of it, Dwight. Tamara's soft voice stabbed at him.

Fighting tears, he scrubbed a hand over his eyes and

inhaled deeply. He didn't want to stop remembering. He didn't want to do anything but stand on the muddy rug, in his wet clothes and think of Tamara.

But he couldn't.

Anna needs you.

He sniffed and wiped his face before he turned back to the woman he'd rescued. Anna lay curled into a fetal position on the couch. It'd been a long, long time since a woman had needed him and though there was nothing sexual about the capacity in which she did, laying hands on her, for any reason, made him uncomfortable. But this need was clear and urgent, a matter of survival rather than desire.

With a swift movement, Dwight shrugged off his jacket, the heavy material landing on the floor with a hushed thud. He could feel the weight of the evening lifting off his shoulders as he did. He then bent slightly, unceremoniously kicking off his boots. They landed with a soft thump. He gathered both the jacket and boots, carrying them over to the door before he strode to the hall closet where the linens were stored. He reached in to pull out a generous armful of thick, comforting blankets.

Returning to Anna's side, he began to layer the blankets over her. His movements were deliberate and gentle, each blanket placed with careful precision. He meticulously tucked in the edges, ensuring no cold air could sneak in and steal away the warmth he was trying to provide.

In his hands, the simple act of covering her with blankets became an almost tender ritual, as he worked to envelop her in a cocoon of warmth. The soft rustle of the blankets seemed to fill the quiet room as he finished, leaving Anna swaddled in a comforting bulwark against the cold.

Next, he headed to the kitchen, filling the teapot with water and setting it atop the stove. The faint hiss of the gas igniting was the only sound in the room as he turned his attention to scouring the cupboards for the hot chocolate packet's Lael kept stocked for Liam.

Finding two, he promptly tore the tops off and emptied their contents into a large mug. The teapot began to whistle, signaling that the water was hot, he filled the mug. Stirring the sweet concoction as he went, he walked back into the living room.

His attention fixated on Anna's parlor and her shallow breaths. She appeared unscathed from what he could see, but was she really okay? What if she had internal injuries, like a punctured lung or a concussion? He knew all too well that some injuries were not visible on the surface. The thought made his stomach churn even more, adding to the knot of worry already forming in his gut.

Maybe he should air on the side of caution, call Copper Creek Rescue and have them snowmobile them to the nearest hospital. And if he was wrong and their injuries weren't life-threatening? He'd be risking the lives of the rescue team.

He'd wait on Lael.

Suddenly, the front door opened. A burst of wind and white proceeded Lael and Liam.

"What happened?" Lael inquired, her gaze intensely fixated on Anna as she quickly removed her hat and coat.

"Their truck slid off the road and ended up in the creek," he explained, cradling the mug in one hand as his other hand gestured toward the bedroom where Hogue was. "The man has an injury to his side. I'm not sure how bad it is, but he's bleeding."

Lael peeled away the blankets to conduct a preliminary examination of Anna. "Her pulse is strong. Are there any visible contusions or lacerations?"

"I'm not sure," Dwight answered.

Lael's brows arched into a frown he recognized as irritation. "Jesus, Dwight," she said, looking under the blankets. "You didn't examine her?"

"I was waiting for you, Lael," he stated, feeling like a scolded boy.

"What were you thinking? That you could just throw a few blankets on the poor woman, and everything would magically be alright?"

"I made hot cocoa for—"

"Quit your stalling," she interrupted, throwing up her hand to shut him up. As she started for the hall, she tossed a command over her shoulder, "Sit that cup down and get her out of those wet clothes."

"Lael," he said, his unusually low voice stern, stalling her exit. "She's a female."

She frowned. "Well, I'm sorry if that makes you uncomfortable."

Dwight knew she wasn't.

"It's simple triage," she told him. "He's bleeding. She's not. I can't be in two places at once. Now, do it."

She made it clear that there was no room for arguments or delays - it was high time for him to step up and do what needed to be done. Lael had always been brutally honest and straight to the point especially when it came to caring for her patients.

Dwight cleared his throat, his eyes shifting to Sonny as he sat the cup on the coffee table in front of the couch.

The man who'd been ramrod for the Sweet Surrender for more than a decade, stood by the door, his eyes reflecting a mix of concern and curiosity. "She doesn't look familiar. Do you know who she is?"

"All I know is that her first name is Anna, and his is Hogue. I suspect that all their belongings, including any form of ID, are still in the truck," Dwight explained.

"Which is probably a mile downstream by now," Sonny added, his tone hinting at the challenges that lay ahead in retrieving it.

Switching topics, Dwight addressed the pack horses. "Bane and Moose are in the barn. Could you see they're taken care of for the night?"

Sonny nodded, his expression serious. "Will do. Anything else?"

Dwight shook his head. "Not at the moment." He was well aware that there was still plenty of work ahead, but for now, they had done all they could.

"Alright then," Sonny said, bracing for the blizzard as he went out the door.

Feeling out of place in his own living room, Dwight rubbed his sweaty palms over his wet, jean-clad thighs and sighed.

Lael was right.

He had to get Anna out of those clothes and into something dry. But first, he had to solve the problem of what she was going to wear.

He hurried down the hall and into his bedroom.

She's my size.

Dwight murmured a quiet "No", dismissing the thought with a shake of his head. Everything in Tamara's closet was exactly as she'd left it the day she'd driven from the ranch and into town - her clothes were arranged by season, color, and purpose. The drawers of her beautifully crafted pine dresser, too, were unchanged. He wouldn't allow a stranger to wear Tamara's things. To him, they were as hallowed as the frozen earth where she now rested.

Instead, he rifled through his dresser, searching for

something he could tie, hang or pin in place long enough for Anna's clothes to dry. One of his faded long-sleeves t-shirts and black and red flannel pajama bottoms would do the trick.

He returned to the living room and saw that she was still in the same position. He couldn't shake off his concern that she might have sustained internal injuries.

Casting aside his own discomfort and qualms about laying his hands on a woman he wasn't intimate with, Dwight knelt beside her.

"Anna?" Dwight's voice was soft but assertive.

There was no response, not even a twitch of her eyelid.

"Anna, it's Dwight. Dwight Murtaugh. You're at the Sweet Surrender Ranch."

Still nothing.

"If you can hear me, I'm going to do a quick check for any injuries."

A soft moan escaped her lips and her eyes fluttered open just a fraction. He cautiously removed her jacket then, gently, he ran his fingers over one arm, searching for any abnormalities. Finding none, he repeated the process with her other arm, still nothing amiss.

What about her head?

Carefully, he slid a hand under the base of her skull and began to feel around. "Nothing. Her head seems alright."

But he couldn't ignore the pale blue tinge on her lips.

She's still so cold, Dwight.

He noticed the small puddles of melted snow on the hardwood floor under Anna's boots, which were hanging off the edge of the couch. The fire warmed the room, but changing into dry clothing would help her body temperature rise faster. "We'll fix that," he said.

He was a man of strong morals, honed by years of his strict upbringing. His regard for others, especially women, was as solid as the stone face of the Rockies. The notion of taking advantage of someone vulnerable was totally foreign to him and preserving Anna's dignity was a priority.

Feeling somewhat clumsy and intrusive, he unzipped her boots, removed them from her feet, and peeled her socks off.

After he'd sat them closer to the fire, he rolled her onto her back and moved to unbuckle the thin belt around her waist. When his fingers grazed the naked flesh of her belly, she let out a soft yelp, flinched and stared despondently up at him with wide eyes.

He wasn't sure if it was the roughness of his fingers or her response to a stranger's touch that caused the reaction, but he had to console her.

"You're safe," he hurried to say. "I'm Dwight, remember? Your truck went over the bank and into the creek. You're soaked."

She blinked lazily and nodded before closing her eyes. Again, her body went limp.

Poor thing. She's exhausted.

He resumed the task, unbuckled her belt, unfastened the snap and unzipped her soaked jeans. He had to lift her slightly to slide them over her hips, noticing as he did, a pair of pink, high-cut panties with delicate lace trim.

A long dormant surge of desire cut through him, provoking heat to coarse through his thawing body and a wave of shame to rock his soul.

It's a natural reaction.

In some instances, so was murder, but he hadn't taken a life.

Oh, Dwight. Don't be such a hard ass.

Tamara could never pull off an expletive and on the rare occasions she tried, he always laughed.

He wasn't laughing now.

God, he missed her.

Swallowing back loss and a swath of emotions, he focused on Anna. He slid the jeans down her legs, taking care to be as gentle and respectful as possible. Each movement was measured and calculated to minimize contact.

His fingers didn't linger. His hands, so accustomed to the gruff handling of ranch work, seemed disproportionately large and clumsy as he delicately maneuvered to remove Anna's arms from the saturated shirt and ease it over her head.

Revealed beneath the discarded shirt was a delicate lacy bra, doing little to hide the soft mounds of her full breasts. The color of the bra matched the enticing pink of her panties, both adorned with an intricate lace pattern.

The combination of softness and strength didn't go unnoticed by Dwight. Laying there clad only in thin lacy undergarments, the woman was a vision of survival, desire and beauty.

He quickly turned his head and took a moment to collect himself. "The underwear stays," he stated firmly, reaching for the t-shirt and pajamas he'd taken from his dresser.

After securing the drawstring of his flannel pajamas around Anna's slender waist, Dwight picked up her wet and dirty clothes from the floor. Once laundered, she'd have something more fitting to wear than a man's over-sized night clothes. He had barely taken a few steps when something slipped from her pocket, striking the wooden floor with a resonant 'ping'. It skittered across the floorboards, coming to rest just a few feet away.

He bent down to retrieve it, his fingers closing around a small object. As he lifted it, the flickering firelight illuminated the lustrous gleam of a simple brass key.

The inconspicuous piece of metal was weightless in his palm, but in his gut, he knew it held a weight that couldn't be measured. Perhaps, hidden within its unassuming form was a story waiting to unfold, a secret yearning to be revealed.

"Snap out of it, Dwight," he mumbled to himself. "You've read too many crime novels."

Maybe he had spent too much time lost in the tattered pages of the dozens of detective fiction books he had shelved in the den. But this was more than a simple lock opener. This key held answers.

He was sure of it.

Chapter Four

The living room was quiet, except for the intermittent crackling of the fire and the palpable pounding of Dwight's heart, resonating loud and clear in his own ears.

He stared down at Anna. The color was returning to her face and lips and she hadn't made a sound in over an hour. He re-situated the blankets with the same care as he had before.

You did good.

"Think so?" he whispered, wishing he had more than a voice to hold on to tonight.

Oh, yes. I'm so proud of you, Dwight.

Tamara had always been an advocate for helping others. Knowing he had acted in a way that would have earned her approval provided a small measure of consolation on a night when he was feeling lonelier than normal.

He took one last glance at Anna before heading to his room to change. There, he shrugged off his wet clothes, replacing them with a dry, warm set of pajamas. He was too exhausted to shower.

Once dressed, Dwight made his way back down the

hall, his steps resonating softly in the quiet house. He stopped at the guest bedroom, the sight of the injured man causing a twinge of concern. "How is he?"

Lael, now nearing her sixties, was a stunning woman. She carried the same distinctive beauty that was so apparent in her daughter. Her expressive blue eyes, often lively and vibrant, were now filled with worry as she tended to Hogue's wound.

Her hair, once a rich chestnut hue, now bore streaks of graceful gray. The soft curves of her face were more pronounced, framed by the subtle lines etched near the edges of her eyes — signs of a life well-lived and a heart that had loved deeply.

Her face was drawn in a mask of concern, her lips pressed into a thin line as she concentrated on her task. Her hands, though steady, betrayed her anxiety with the occasional tremor. The sight of her so worried only added to Dwight's own unease.

"He's stable for now," she finally said, but didn't look up from her task, her focus solely on the man lying unconscious on the bed. "But this looks like a bullet wound."

"He's been shot?" Dwight repeated, his tone laced with disbelief as he bent down to lift a dozing Liam from a nearby chair and into his arms. His mind was suddenly abuzz with a flurry of questions. How had Hogue ended up with a bullet wound? Who was responsible? And most importantly, why were the two of them doing so far off the main road? In a snowstorm? Had they gotten lost? Or were they on the run?

Told you so. Tamara took every opportunity to remind him she was right.

"And that's not the worst of it," Lael confirmed, her eyes meeting his briefly before returning to her patient.

"I didn't find an exit wound. I'm no surgeon, Dwight. This man needs a hospital. Call Nolan."

Nolan Blackfeather, the town sheriff, was the obvious choice to handle the gunshot wound. But as Dwight looked around the room - at Hogue lying on the bed, bandaged and weak, Lael nursing him with such devotion, Anna sleeping soundly in the next room, and Liam cradled protectively in his arms - he couldn't help but wish that this call could wait. That they were all safe within the walls of the ranch. But it was clear that Hogue was running out of time.

"I'll make the call." Dwight headed out of the guest bedroom and up the stairs to put Liam in his bed. As he carried the drowsy boy towards his room, he stared down at his son. With his tousled red hair and round cherubic face, was the spitting image of his mother. His tiny hands clung to Dwight's shirt, his breaths soft and rhythmic against his chest.

Liam was everything to him. The one bright spot in his otherwise bleak existence. As he cradled his slumbering son, a fierce protectiveness rose inside of him. He would do anything, fight anyone, to keep Liam safe and shielded from the harsh reality of the world. Nothing would ever come between them.

He carefully laid the boy in his bed, tucking him in snugly with the dinosaur quilt. Liam's lids parted sleepily. "G'night, Daddy."

Dwight's heart swelled with an overwhelming wave of love as he gazed down at his son. The boy's face, with its delicate features and soft skin, was like a beautiful painting that captured all the love he and Tamara had shared. Liam held Dwight's heart in his small hands, and he knew without a doubt that this was his greatest treasure. In this moment, looking into those trusting and loving eyes, everything else faded away and only the pure innocence and joy of life remained. "Night, son."

The little one's face was serene as he drifted back to sleep.

Closing the door behind him, he hurried back downstairs to dial the sheriff's cell phone. He'd had the number on speed dial since Tamara's accident.

"Dwight," Nolan's low voice answered. "I hope this is a social call."

"I wish it was."

"What's going on?"

"Long story short," Dwight said, tucking his free hand under his armpit as Lael joined him in the hallway. "I have a woman on my couch nearly frozen to death and a man in my guest bedroom with a bullet in his side."

"Tonight keeps getting better and better," Nolan said, sighing heavily.

An eerie feeling swept over Dwight. "Meaning?"

"There was an avalanche at Stone Point this afternoon." Nestled deep in the rugged mountains of Copper Creek, lay Stone Point Ski Resort. A perilous paradise for thrill-seekers, luring them with its challenging slopes and panoramic vistas. But danger loomed in the resort's picturesque landscape. Its high altitude and treacherous terrain made it a prime target for deadly avalanches, lurking just beneath the surface, waiting to strike at any moment.

"We have three missing skiers and all personnel out there looking for them," Nolan explained. "And more than two dozen injured, some seriously. All of our medics are up to their elbows in contusions and broken bones. We have a canine unit on the way, but they won't be here until tomorrow."

"Damn." Dwight shook his head.

"I'm sorry, but I'm afraid it'll be morning before I can get someone out there."

"What did he say?" Lael asked, tugging at Dwight's shirtsleeve.

"An avalanche," he relayed the message. "They can't get here until morning."

Lael, wearing a worried expression, headed back to the guest bedroom to check on Hogue.

"Let me know if anything changes," Nolan said. "Otherwise, I'll see you in the morning."

Unwilling to surrender to his own need for rest, Dwight wandered back into the living room. He poured himself a stiff drink, the amber liquid swirling in the glass as he contemplated the night's events. His hand was steady as he lifted the glass, taking a slow sip of the strong liquor, feeling the burn of it as it slid down his throat.

Settling into a chair by the fire, the familiar hint of cedar caught Dwight's nose. He took a deep breath and tasted the air, finding it tinged with cinnamon from the piece of uneaten apple pie Lael had left for him. It mingled with the smokiness to create an ambience that was distinctly home. Before he'd lost Tamara, those scents had carried with it the promise of a satisfying supper and a long romantic night with his wife. Now, it was just another reminder of what he'd lost.

He shifted in his chair, the soft leather creaking under his weight, and stretched out his long legs towards the fire, feeling the heat seep into the soles of his feet and warming them thoroughly. The comforting sizzle and pop of burning logs played a tune for him alone, punctuating the silence of the room like an old familiar song.

His focus shifted to Anna. In a small way, he was thankful for the interruption she'd caused in his routine life. Watching her chest rise and fall in the rhythmic pattern of sleep, seeing the stress lines on her face at ease made him feel pretty damn good.

Helping Anna hadn't mended his broken heart. Nothing or no one ever would but rescuing her had certainly made the weight of his loss slightly more bearable, at least for tonight. The knowledge that he was carrying on Tamara's legacy of kindness made him feel a little less shattered.

ANNA WAS ACCUSTOMED TO NIGHTMARES, false realities evoked by the frail psyche of a child tossed on the winds of the foster care system all those years ago and her most recent source of terror — the tangible nightmare of being face to face with evil.

She opened her eyes to a wooden ceiling. That wasn't a figment of a nightmarish dream, nor were the scent of wood and smoke, or the warmth radiating towards her feet, casting an unfamiliar yet utterly comforting sense of security through her body. She blinked, snuggling deeper into the blanket draped over her as memories of John's murder and her spontaneous drive to Montana resurfaced.

She and Hogue had been en route to the Brewster Ranch when the snow started to fall, making her take a wrong turn. The hill. She'd skidded off the road and into the water. What had transpired after that? How had she and Hogue managed to escape her truck? The creek? Thinking for a second, she began to remember. There was a man.

A cowboy. He'd rescued them.

Anna propped herself up on one elbow and surveyed her surroundings, half afraid that maybe she'd been wrong and that the one part of last night's ordeal had been a figment of her imagination.

Her eyes scanned the dimly lit room, searching, hoping...

There, in a recliner across from her, he lay. A shirtless hero sleeping peacefully. In the soft light, she admired his rugged features: a few days' worth of stubble outlining a chiseled jawline, tousled dark hair that only added to his untamed sex appeal. Even with his eyes closed, she could feel the intensity of his deep blue eyes. Those were now eternally etched into her memory.

Dwight. A sense of relief washed over her by his presence. Why? She wasn't sure. Her heart was still entangled in the bitter tendrils of grief, mourning the man she thought she'd loved wholly and fiercely. The man she'd once envisioned a life with.

So why did the sight of this man, her unexpected savior, fill her with such a strange sense of comfort? Why did this cowboy, who had yanked her away from the jaws of death, cause her heart to flutter in a way she thought it had forgotten?

Her gaze moved to his hand resting on the recliner arm. Large and masculine. Yet, careful, and gentle as he'd removed her wet clothing and felt for injuries.

Wait. What?

Anna jerked the blankets up, only to find she was wearing someone else's clothes. "Oh, dear," she whispered, remembering vague moments of conciseness when the warmth of his hands had brushed over her cold skin.

Dwight stirred, lifting his head and blinking away the remnants of sleep from his eyes. "You're awake," he stated, his voice a low rumble that resonated in the quiet room.

"Yes," she said. "Sorry. I-I didn't mean to disturb you."

With a gruff sigh that seemed to carry the weight of the world, he pushed the footrest down with a soft mechanical whisper and sat up, his movements so fluid they belied his size. He ran a hand over his scruffy jawline, the coarse bristles rasping under his palm, a sound barely audible yet distinctly felt in the charged silence of the room. "It's alright," he assured her, his voice a low rumble that vibrated through her chest, rising to his full impressive height with an aura of authority that seemed as natural to him as breathing.

He rose, unfolding from the chair with an aura of authority that seemed to fill the space, displacing air as if he were a force of nature. Light from the fire cast golden warmth across his handsome face and highlighted the blue in his eyes like flecks of glass.

His bare chest, covered in a thin layer of dark hair, held her attention, doing something strange to her insides. It was a strange, fluttering sensation she wasn't ready to identify.

As the fog of confusion and male appreciation cleared from her addled brain, her concern centered on Hogue. "How is he?"

Crouching to one knee, Dwight began stoking the fire. "Resting in the guest bedroom."

Anna tossed back the mound of blankets covering her and sat up. "I need to see him."

"Why? So you can come up with a believable story for the bullet wound gouged into his side?" His voice remained low and casual, but there was an underlying tone of doubt that reverberated off the walls.

"What? No!" Her response came out a little too quickly, her voice slightly defensive. But she couldn't deny that what Dwight suggested made sense. So far, neither she nor Hogue had given substantial thought to the inevitable questions they would face once they reached Copper Creek.

The bullet wound was a damning piece of evidence, etched into the flesh and blood of the man who had raised her. It was a story she wasn't ready to tell, but for John's sake, the truth would have to be revealed eventually. The consequences of her actions couldn't be avoided forever.

But how to spin a tale that could explain a bullet wound without revealing the grim reality that lay behind it? A truth that could endanger not just them, but also the man who had unknowingly walked into their nightmare.

"Anna!" She heard Hogue's frail voice ring out.

With a surge of adrenaline, she sprang to her feet. Her body protested the abrupt movement, still recovering from the icy grip of near-hypothermia. Drained from exhaustion and weakened by days without a decent meal, she felt a wave of dizziness wash over her. Yet, her focus was on Hogue. He needed her.

She attempted to take a step forward, but her feet were unexpectedly trapped within the tumble of blankets that had slipped unnoticed to the floor. The sudden constraint, paired with her already shaky state, amplified her disorientation, causing the room to spin around her in a dizzying whirl.

"Whoa, there," Dwight commanded softly, coming to her side.

"I'm fine, really," she assured him, feeling more breathless and dizzy now that he was touching her. "Where is he?"

With a gentle but firm grip on her elbow, he deftly removed the tangled blankets from her feet and guided her down the hall to the guest bedroom. "I'll be in the kitchen," he murmured, his voice deep and reassuring as he left her to visit.

Hogue lay on a large, hand-hewn bed, his complexion a blunt contrast against the colorful and carefully stitched quilt. His skin, usually weathered and bronzed, now looked pale and fragile.

The room was filled with the sound of his labored breathing, each exhalation a reminder of the painful ordeal they had survived. Through tired eyes, he looked up at her and smiled. "Annie."

Memories came rushing back to her, each one a poignant reminder of the happiest years of her life. Times during her childhood, being tossed around from one foster home to another, feeling lost and unwanted until she found refuge in the Brewster home.

Warm tears welled up in her eyes and spilled over, trickling down her cheeks. She'd lost John and now Hogue, her only family, was battling for his life in a stranger's house. And it was all her fault. The sob that rose in her throat was a raw, primal sound that filled the cozy bedroom.

"I'm so sorry, Hogue." Her hand shook with a cocktail of remorse and self-loathing as she grasped onto his, clinging to the final shreds of hope she had left. He had been more than just a foster parent to her; he was like the steady lighthouse guiding her through the stormy waves of every hardship.

"Hush now," he ordered. "It was an accident."

Guilt weighed heavily upon Anna's conscience, threatening to consume her entirely. She'd always been known for her gentleness and kindness, but now she couldn't escape the sting of remorse. How could she have betrayed Hogue, the man who had given her such cherished childhood memories?

Her moral compass was shattered, leaving her lost in

a sea of uncertainty. How could she ever make amends for the pain she'd inflicted upon someone she loved so dearly? Only time would tell if her heart could ever find peace again.

"Remember what we talked about? Our plan?" His voice, weak but warm, was just a soft scrap against the air. A frail smile played at the corners of his mouth.

Anna could feel the weight of those words. It was more than just a plan; it was a future they dared to dream.

She couldn't shake the feeling that Dwight was lurking in the shadows of the hallway, eavesdropping on their conversation, and searching for answers she refused to give. Was he watching them now, his mind racing with suspicions and questions? She could practically feel distrust oozing from him, amplified by Hogue's injury. Paranoia or not, she wasn't taking any chances with Dwight overhearing her discussion with Hogue.

"Don't speak now," she urged him in a gentle whisper. "You need to rest. We can discuss our plan when you're stronger." The plan — an ambiguous arrangement they had hatched, a strategy for the future that was as nebulous as it was optimistic. But now wasn't the time to dwell on it.

"Hush, girl," he chided her softly, the way he always had, with a tenderness that was far removed from the harsh discipline of her previous foster homes. "We both know I've got more time behind me than I do in front of me, even without the bullet."

The hard reality of his words stung. It was a truth she had always avoided thinking about. Hogue and Martha, already in the autumn of their lives, had welcomed her into their home two decades ago. "Don't say that," she pleaded, fighting back the torrent of tears that threatened to spill over.

"You were always such a tender-hearted soul," he murmured, reaching up to tenderly stroke her cheek. "You've blossomed into a remarkable woman." His voice wavered, thick with emotion. "Martha would be bursting with pride. I know I am. I love you, Annie."

"I love you too," she whispered back, pressing a kiss to his worn hand before gently placing it on the bed. The uncertainty of what lay ahead, the possibility of losing the only family she had left filled her with a dread she dared not voice. She was left with the remnants of their plan, a plan that felt as delicate and uncertain as the man lying before her.

"How's our patient doing?" The question, soft but firm, drifted into the room from the doorway. Her very essence exuded comfort and compassion, filling the room with an overwhelming sense of peace.

Her hair, a beautiful blend of silver and brown, was pulled back in a loose ponytail, a few strands escaping to frame her face. Her eyes, the color of a stormy sky, were affectionate yet piercing, holding a depth that spoke of wisdom gained from years of experience. There was something in her gaze, a mix of empathy and resilience, that put Anna at ease instantly as she approached the bed to take Hogue's pulse.

Her hands, though slightly aged and lined, radiated a strength that was soothing. They were the hands of a caregiver, hands that had comforted many in pain, hands that were about to extend the same care to Hogue.

Dwight, who had been silent till now, cleared his throat and introduced her. "Anna, this is Lael, my mother-in-law."

A jolt of surprise hit her like a lightning bolt. The revelation that he had a mother-in-law – that he was tied to another woman – blindsided her, sending an unexpected surge of unease through her veins. With the grace of someone who'd perfected the art of hiding emotions, she kept her expression serene, even as this bombshell rattled her to her core. Inside, though, a storm brewed; confusion and disquiet twisted together in a relentless churn. It was a reaction she couldn't fully grasp, an intricate web of feelings that left her on edge and bewildered.

Anna stood up from the bed, her arms reaching out for Lael in a warm embrace. She couldn't thank this woman enough. Lael had selflessly cared for Hogue and without a doubt, saved his life. "Thank you, Lael," Anna's voice dripped with genuine emotion that threatened to overflow. "For helping Hogue," she managed to choke out, her words filled with profound appreciation.

"Oh, honey. You're welcome." Lael returned Anna's hug with warmth, before pulling back to study her face with a discerning gaze. "When's the last time you ate?"

Anna thought for a minute, her mind racing to recall their last proper meal. The past few days had been a blur of adrenaline, fear, and relentless driving since their hasty escape from Malachi in Colorado. Meals had become an afterthought during their flight from Harmony, their sustenance derived from whatever quick snacks they could grab at gas stations along their way.

"We managed some doughnuts yesterday," she admitted. "And jerky, I think, the day before that."

A frown creased Lael's forehead. "Well, we can't have that." She wrapped an arm around Anna's shoulders, guiding her towards the hall. "Come on. Let's get some real food in you."

"But Hogue—"

"I'll get changed and check in on him before I head out," Dwight's voice cut through her protest, calm and assured. "We'll be digging out from under the snow for a couple of days," he had said, his words painting a vivid image of the grueling physical labor that was a rancher's lot – the ceaseless battle against nature, the early mornings spent in the biting cold, the long nights that stretched on under the weight of responsibility.

But along with the tasks that awaited him, Dwight stood there, extending a helping hand, offering comfort where he could. His kindness filled Anna's heart, stirring a gratitude so deep and pure it felt like a balm to her weary soul.

Chapter Five

Dwight had come to terms with the sleepless nights, the bad dreams that left him gasping in the darkness, calling out Tamara's name. But what he couldn't get used to was the hollowness that awaited him each morning. The gut punch of waking up to an empty bed, the crushing truth that Tamara was gone.

These days, he dressed in solitude within the confines of their once-shared bedroom. The room, alive with their laughter and whispers of love, now echoed with the deafening silence of her absence. The vacant spot next to him in bed and the untouched pillow, served a constant reminder of the void she'd left behind.

He remembered the morning rush, the good-natured battle for the bathroom sink, the playful dodges and turns in front of the mirror. Those once annoying morning routines had become so precious to him now and were moments he'd give anything to relive.

As he stood before the mirror, combing his hair, he could almost see her next to him. Those were the times when a simple brush of the arm, a quick catch of the eye, could turn into something more. Something intimate and special, stolen moments of love in the quiet before dawn.

His reflection stared back at him, a single figure in the mirror. An emptiness beside him where Tamara once stood, her laughter and smiles just a phantom now. He longed for her, for those days, for the love that once filled this room. Each morning was a reminder of what had been, amplifying the silence that now ruled.

But this morning was different. He woke up to a new reality, one where another woman - Anna - was in his house. She was sitting comfortably at Tamara's table, eating food made by Tamara's mom. The whole thing felt wrong, like he was looking at a picture that was somehow off. Like he'd defiled his late wife's memory'.

The feeling of guilt was hard to shake off. He was irritated that he was expected to play the good host, the friendly neighbor. He didn't feel like being nice. But he also felt bad for not wanting to be those things. After all, Anna was a stranger who had nearly lost her life.

However, he couldn't ignore the alarm bells ringing in his head. Anna and Hogue's sudden appearance, the mysterious gunshot wound, their unexpected arrival in the middle of a snowstorm - it all reeked of danger and deceit. He was determined to uncover the truth, to understand why they had shown up at his ranch.

Despite his doubts, he knew he'd have to keep up appearances. Lael would make sure of that. He would have to play the hospitable host, even if his mind was filled with questions and suspicions. His home, once a peaceful sanctuary, now felt like a stage for a drama he hadn't agreed to be part of and one that wasn't going to end well.

And he wasn't happy about any of it. Not one damn bit.

Dwight reached into his closet, pulling out one of his flannel shirts. The fabric was warm and familiar against his skin as he slipped it on and readied himself for the day ahead. The delicious scent of bacon and eggs wafted from the kitchen and he knew a steaming cup of coffee was waiting for him. It was a routine morning, or as routine as it could get with strangers in his home.

As he buttoned up his shirt, he remembered his promise to Anna - to check in on Hogue. After quietly descending the stairs, he headed for the guest bedroom. He pushed the door open and peeked inside. The stillness of the room was unsettling, broken only by the shallow, barely noticeable measure of Hogue's chest moving up and down.

He stepped further in, the wooden floorboards creaking beneath his weight. The closer he got, the more his concern grew. Hogue's breathing was labored, each breath seeming to take a monumental effort. Dwight found himself holding his own breath, his gaze fixed on the frail and ghostly white parlor of the man.

Every instinct in him screamed that something wasn't right. The room was filled with an uneasy silence, the air heavy with a sense of foreboding. It was as though time had slowed down, each second stretching out as he watched, his heart pounding in his chest, hoping to see the reassuring rise and fall of Hogue's breath.

Dwight reached out, his hand hovering for a moment before gently touching the man's shoulder. "Hogue?" he called out softly. His eyelids fluttered open, but there was a distant look in his eyes that coiled dread in Dwight's stomach. A veil was lifting, a transition from life to death was taking place right before his eyes. This was it—Hogue was slipping away.

"He'll be coming for her," Hogue managed to say, his voice barely audible.

Dwight's skin prickled with unease. Even on the brink of death, Hogue was issuing a warning.

He pressed, "Who, Hogue? Who's coming for Anna?"

"Got to...protect her," he gasped, his breath growing shallower with each passing moment.

"I will," Dwight promised, his voice steady despite the uneasiness inside him.

With a surprising burst of strength, Hogue's frail hand reached up and grabbed Dwight's shirt. His grip was firm, insistent. "Promise me."

"You have my word, Hogue."

And with that, Hogue's grip slackened. His hand fell lifeless against the cool sheets of the bed. His breathing, erratic and shallow, ended with one last, uneven gasp. And just like that, he was no more.

"Shit," Dwight muttered under his breath. He took a seat at the end of the bed, the weight of the promise he'd just made settling heavily on his shoulders. Placing his elbows on his knees, he rested his head in his hands.

The muffled sounds of conversation and laughter filtered through from the kitchen. Dwight could hear Anna and Lael chatting, their voices soft and filled with warmth. They were oblivious to the grim news he was about to deliver. How was he going to break it to Anna that Hogue was gone?

Her affection for the man had been evident in every interaction they'd had. The way her eyes lit up when she spoke to him, the gentle way she cared for his wounds, the worry lines that creased her forehead whenever he winced in pain. It was clear that she had a deep bond with the man, a love that was as palpable as it was profound.

Dwight could almost see the scene play out in his mind. The laughter would die down, replaced by a mournful hush. Anna's face would fall, her eyes welling up with tears. The kitchen, moments ago a place of warmth and lively conversation, would turn into a room filled with grief and loss.

He was overcome with a sick feeling that reminded him of the night the sheriff had knocked on his door, telling him that Tamara was gone. He could still remember the pained expression on Nolan's face, the way his voice had shook as he broke the news. It was a night when Dwight's world had been turned upside down.

Now, he was faced with the task of causing the same kind of pain to Anna. He inhaled deeply, steeling himself for the difficult conversation ahead. Just as he was mustering up the courage to rise, the bedroom door creaked open. Anna walked in, her hands carefully balancing a tray piled high with food, no doubt prepared lovingly for Hogue.

She stopped abruptly, her gaze darting from Hogue's lifeless body to Dwight's somber face.

Dwight slowly rose to his feet. "I-I'm sorry, Anna," he stuttered, his voice laden with a sorrow he couldn't hide.

Her face crumpled, the weight of reality crashing down on her. "No!" she cried out, the tray slipping from her grasp and clattering loudly on the floor.

Overwhelmed with grief, Anna's knees buckled, and she collapsed. Swiftly, Dwight caught her before she hit the floor. He scooped her up and made his way out of the room.

"He's gone," he informed Lael as they crossed paths in the hallway. He carried Anna to the living room, her body shaking with sobs against his chest. It was a strange feeling, having her in his arms for the second time in a matter of hours.

Only moments ago, he'd been wrestling with his irritation at having to be pleasant to her. Now, with her tears soaking his shirt and her heartache palpable in her every breath, he felt a strange mix of sadness, empathy, and a lingering trace of that initial irritation. It was a confusing cocktail of emotions that left him feeling more out of sorts than ever.

With Anna cradled in his arms, Dwight sank down onto the couch, all too aware of the profound sorrow that was shaking her body. Her cries were heartbreakingly raw, the kind of sorrowful wails only deep, unrelenting grief could invoke. It was a gut-wrenching loss that Dwight was all too familiar with.

He could feel her tears seeping through his shirt, each one proof of her pain and there was something else in the air too, something other than anguish. It was something ominous. Danger. He could almost taste it, a lurking threat that was just as real as the heartache Anna was experiencing.

He didn't know what it was or where it was coming from and though he'd made a promise to comfort a dying man, he felt something rise inside of him. A steadfast and burning need to protect the woman in his arms.

"I'VE GIVEN HER A SEDATIVE."

Dwight watched Lael tuck Anna in, her actions gentle, like a mother with her child. "She'll sleep until supper, at least."

Dwight's gaze moved to Anna's face, pale against the dark leather couch, but she finally looked at peace. He knew that would change when she woke up and faced the reality of Hogue's death.

Supper was still a whole eight hours away, a stretch that felt daunting in its uncertainty. A lot could happen in that amount of time. The thought pricked at his worry, but he pushed it aside. They had some breathing room, at least until Nolan arrived and the questions started.

"He should be here by then," Dwight murmured. His words meant more for his own ears than for Lael's. He wasn't a man who jumped at shadows and unfamiliar noises and, knowing that Sheriff Nolan Blackfeather was on his way, didn't exactly bring Dwight comfort. But it did make him feel a little more at ease about the things he didn't know. The sheriff had resources and investigative capabilities that Dwight lacked.

Nolan could dig into Anna and Hogue's pasts, uncover the hidden layers that Dwight didn't have the means to access.

But with the thought of the sheriff's arrival, a new worry began to gnaw at Dwight. Nolan would undoubtedly have questions, a lot of them, questions that needed answers to make sense of the situation.

A man was dead, complications from a gunshot wound.

Yeah, Dwight thought to himself as he scrubbed a hand over his eyes. They'd most certainly be questions. And the person with those answers was now deep in a sedative-induced sleep.

"Here." He looked down when he felt Lael nudge his arm and handed him a worn, water-damaged wallet. Surprised the creek hadn't washed it away, he opened it to find several cards and cash, including a driver's license. He took it and opened the trifold, revealing multiple laminated cards, one of which was a driver's license. "Hogue Edison Brewster."

"I didn't know Ronnie had any family left," she said, peering over Dwight's shoulder to look at the contents of the wallet.

"Me neither."

There were a few outdated credit cards and some

cash, but nothing worth getting shot for. But then again, criminals didn't need much motivation.

Lael's curiosity got the best of her as she pointed to a small slip of paper peeking out from the thin lining of his wallet. "What's that?"

"I'm not sure." Easing it out, he retrieved the wet paper and handed her back the wallet, his attention now solely on the delicate mystery. He unfolded it and its purpose was clear. The hidden paper was Hogue's last will and testament leaving everything to Anna, including the Brewster ranch.

Lael let out a soft whistle. "Well, there you have it."

He frowned. "Have what? All this tells us is that she's the new owner of one dilapidated ranch house and overgrown pasture land."

Lael shrugged, indifferent to the fact. "It'll be nice having a neighbor again."

Dwight rubbed his jaw. "A neighbor, Lael? That's all you can say?"

She rested a fist on her hip and gave him a cool stare. "I'm just trying to look on the bright side of things, Dwight. That's all. It wouldn't kill you to do the same every once in a while."

He scoffed and shook his head. "There is no bright side to this. It's going to end bad. I can feel it in my bones."

"Pftt," she replied, passing his uneasiness off. "That's arthritis."

Dwight knew the difference between achy joints and intuition, but all they could do was wait for Nolan to arrive. Maybe by then, Anna would be awake and willing to talk.

He let out a sigh, his gaze drifting toward the window and the world outside. With the sunrise, a sea of blue skies and bright sunshine had washed over the

Sweet Surrender, transforming the snow-covered landscape into a dazzling spectacle of light and shadow. The storm had relinquished its grip, sheathed the world in a glittering, icy armor. Their connection to the rest of Copper Creek was severed, leaving them marooned in a frosty solitude.

Given Hogue's eerie warning, Dwight couldn't help but see that as perhaps a silver lining. The raging blizzard they'd survived last night had become a protective barrier of sorts, shielding them from unseen dangers.

"What's really on your mind?"

He let out another long sigh and turned to face Lael. "You mean other than the obvious?"

"You haven't stared out that window since Tamara died. What are you not telling me?"

He hadn't told her about Hogue's last words. There was no need to worry her, but he knew he couldn't keep what might be coming a secret from her forever. Stalling was his best bet. Lael was no fool. "Nolan is going to have questions."

"I'm sure he will."

He looked at Anna, her peaceful slumber tugging at his heartstrings. Another surge of protectiveness washed over him. "He'll want to question her."

"That's usually the way these things go, Dwight."

"Ah, hell, Lael," he said, sliding his hands into his pockets. "I just worry it might be too much for her at this point." He shrugged, adding, "You know how Nolan can be."

Lael let out a derisive snort. "He does have a knack for coming off as tough."

"Especially to those unfamiliar with his particular brand of charm," Dwight added, dryly.

She narrowed her eyes at him. "So, what's your point?"

"I just thought that maybe you, being her primary caregiver, suggest Nolan might ask his questions later, after Anna's had time to recover."

A coy smile spread across Lael's face. "Ah. I see."

Dwight hoped she didn't because how hard Nolan questioned Anna shouldn't concern him, but it did.

And he didn't know why. All he did know was that he was a man of his word and he'd keep her safe from whatever was coming, and he'd do so without breaking his marriage vows.

"LAST NAME?" The question reverberated through Anna's mind as she struggled to force her eyelids apart.

Lael must have given her a strong dose of something, because all she could see were faint slits of light. Gradually, her vision returned to normal and her senses began to awaken. She noticed the soft glow of the setting sun shining through the window and the shadows growing longer in the room. It was dusk, another day gone by while she slept. Luckily, there were no nightmares this time; just blissful darkness. As she slowly regained her bearings, she saw Dwight exchanging something with a man at the front door, which made her feel uneasy and disoriented.

"The name on his license says Hogue Brewster," Dwight filled in.

The words hit Anna like a sledgehammer, her heart splintering into a thousand pieces all over again. Hogue was dead and by her hand. Her eyes filled with tears, blurring her already hazy vision as she tried to make out the man Dwight and Lael were speaking to.

His presence was commanding, his skin a deep bronze that spoke of a bond with the rugged earth. His eyes were dark and focused. His face was chiseled and strong, marked by prominent cheekbones and framed by long, straight hair.

His attire was perfectly suited for the cold outside - a sturdy, dark blue winter jacket, black snow pants, and solid winter boots. And there was a gold star embroidered on his jacket.

He was a lawman.

A lump formed in Anna's throat as realization dawned. Dwight had called the authorities. Oh, God.

"Any relation to Ronnie Brewster?" the lawman asked as he inspected Hogue's license. "You're deceased neighbor?"

"He didn't say, Sheriff, but," Dwight crossed his arms over his chest and sighed. "I'm thinking there's a good probability Hogue was Ronnie's brother."

The sheriff stuffed the license into the inside pocket of his jacket. "Did he say who shot him?"

Both Dwight and Lael shook their heads no.

"And her?" the man nodded towards Anna, causing sheer panic to envelope her. "Do you know anything other than her first name?"

Again, they indicated they didn't.

"Right." He twisted his mouth to one side, considering his options. "You know," he said, narrowing his eyes in Dwight's direction. "This would be a lot easier if I could speak to her."

When the sheriff turned his attention towards Anna, the fear inside her escalated. She was an unknown person here, with nothing but a first name to her credit.

"True," Dwight said. "But Lael gave her a sedative to help her rest."

"It could be awhile before she's coherent enough to answer questions," Lael added.

The sheriff shrugged. "I can wait."

"Look, Nolan," Dwight said, taking a deep breath that expanded his chest. "It's obvious she's not going anywhere. Her truck is at the bottom of the creek and trust me when I say, she can't ride a horse worth a damn."

Nolan was quiet for a couple of minutes, then he pulled Dwight off to the side. They were out of Lael's hearing range, but Anna could still hear their conversation. "You okay, Dwight?"

Dwight frowned. "Yeah. Why?"

Nolan dipped his head. "I know things have been rough since Tamara's passing."

At the mention of the woman's name, Anna saw Dwight's back stiffen and his expression harden. "Don't."

"I'm saying this as a friend," the sheriff told him as he lowered his voice. "But you can't let yourself get caught up in whatever trouble this woman is in. She isn't your responsibility. You don't have to protect her."

"I'm not," Dwight assured him, his jaw clenching tight.

"It's been two years." Nolan placed a firm grip on Dwight's shoulder. "I know you feel guilty that you weren't driving that night, but—"

"Goddamn it, Nolan" Dwight seethed, shrugging off the man's hand. "Is that what you think? That I'm protecting this woman because I couldn't help my wife?"

Anna's gaze shifted to the wedding photos adorning the mantel, capturing moments of pure joy and promises of forever. Dwight and Tamara's smiles, frozen in time, seemed to whisper tales of love that transcended earthly bounds. Nearby, a collection of pregnancy photos nestled in a frame, a witness to the dreams they once shared of a family that now existed only in memories.

She closed her eyes tight as images of Dwight's heroic actions from last night flashed through her mind. His words as he held her tightly in his arms, *Oh, my sweet Tamara. I've got you. You're safe, honey. You're safe.* That's why he'd been dead set on saving her from the icy clutches of the creek.

A hard knot of understanding formed in Anna's stomach. Dwight's wife had died in an automobile accident.

A part of Anna's soul still mourned for John. But she couldn't ignore the bond that was forming with Dwight. Maybe it was their shared history of loving deeply, losing painfully, and striving to carry on despite the gaping void left in their hearts.

"All I'm saying is guilt can make a man crazy," the sheriff replied, his tone low and laden with empathy. "And you don't know this woman. She could be an axe murder for all we know."

Dwight's face went deadpan. "I'll have Sonny hide all the axes. There. Are you happy now?"

The sheriff, knowing he wasn't getting anywhere with his friend, turned and walked to the front door. "I'll have my deputy take the body to the morgue and I'll be back to question her."

Chapter Six

THE LARGE DEPOSITS OF SNOW THAT HAD fallen overnight had transformed the landscape into a pristine white wonderland, with drifts of snow piling up in magnificent heaps.

Dwight, undeterred by the weather and needing answers, decided it was time to venture out into the cold. His mission was to locate Anna's truck, which he hoped hadn't been swept away by the swift current of the creek. He held onto a glimmer of hope that he might recover some of her belongings from the wreckage and something, anything, that might help him learn more about who his houseguest was.

Anna hadn't said more than a half a dozen words since Hogue's passing, choosing instead to sit alone by the window. Dwight didn't know who or what she was looking for as she stared at the snow-covered vistas of the Rockies, but he knew the loss reflected in her eyes. He also knew no amount of talking would help her. She needed time to heal, time to accept the loss, and time to move on.

The sun radiated off the pristine, powdery snow, creating a breathtaking white landscape. The sky was a flawless painting of vibrant blue, reaching endlessly into the distance only broken by the peeking tops of majestic trees covered in a layer of fluffy snow.

Despite the radiant sunshine, the day was biting cold. The chill hung in the air, nipping at his exposed skin and making his breath visible with each exhale. Bane, strong and steady, trudged through the snow.

Now and then, a gust of wind would pick up, stirring the snow into a flurry of sparkling particles that danced in the sunlight before settling back down.

Dwight found the truck not far from where it had been swept away. The once durable vehicle was now a pitiful sight, having been pushed downstream by the swift current. It had come to rest a hundred yards or so from where it went in, cradled awkwardly by a huddle of large, frost-covered rocks on the opposite bank.

Guiding Bane, he carefully navigated upstream, searching for a spot where the water was calm and shallow enough to cross without drenching himself. He found a place where the current slowed, the water pooling into a shallow, serene patch within the otherwise turbulent creek. With a nudge, Dwight urged the horse forward, crossing without trouble to the other side.

As he approached the truck, a wave of uneasiness and anxiety washed over him, not only because of what had happened two nights ago but also because a part of him knew Nolan was right.

When he first locked eyes with the terrified woman in the truck, he hadn't seen a stranger. For a split second, he'd seen the wide, fearful gaze of Tamara. He blamed himself for his wife's death and maybe, just maybe, he saw a chance for redemption by helping Anna.

He turned his face towards the sun, closed his eyes and took a deep breath, needing to hear Tamara's voice, that everything was going to be okay, that he was doing the right thing, but there was only silence.

He could always hear Tamara.

Always.

What the hell was going on? "Talk to me, honey," he whispered.

Again, silence.

Dwight opened his eyes, resolving to the possibility that he might never hear his wife's voice again. He pushed aside the surge of fresh heartbreak the thought brought with it, focusing instead on the task at hand - salvaging what he could from the remnants of Anna's belongings.

The truck's faded blue paint was marred with scratches and chips, the raw metal beneath exposed to the elements. It bore the scars of its recent tumble down the steep slope. The windshield was cracked, a spiderweb of shattered glass that reflected the sunlight in a thousand tiny prisms.

The tires, which looked to be worn and without treads, were now deflated and lifeless. They sagged under the weight of the truck. The rims dug into the rocky earth, holding the vehicle in place on the icy bank.

The most glaring damage, however, was the missing back glass. The void, the result of Dwight's powerful kick that had shattered the surface into a thousand pieces.

Nimbly, he maneuvered his way across the uneven terrain, leaping from rock to rock until he reached the truck. He hoisted himself up and climbed into the bed, his boots crunching on the shattered glass that littered the metal surface.

He'd expected to find luggage or duffle bags, signs of a road trip or a life in transition. But all he found was a waterlogged leather purse nestled in a mound of creek mud beneath the steering wheel.

He crawled through the rear window and retrieved the purse. As he lifted it, water cascaded from its interior, falling in a pitter-patter onto the muddy floor of the cab.

Unzipping the bag, he sifted through its contents: a cell phone, a small hairbrush still adorned with strands of wet hair, a bottle of sanitizer, a tube of hand lotion, and finally, a leather wallet. As he unfolded the wallet, three one-dollar bills, damp and crumpled, fell out, along with a driver's license.

He picked it up, his fingers brushing against the laminated card. Anna Sumner, the name read, followed by an address: 1489 Wallace Street, Harmony, Colorado. As he read the details, a sense of reality set in - Anna Sumner had left Colorado in a hurry, with minimal cash in her wallet and a single key and he needed to know why.

DWIGHT'S pajamas were made of a soft fabric that felt like a warm hug, enveloping her in comfort. The sleeves were too long for her arms, and the pants were far too big for her legs - a clear indication of how much bigger and stronger Dwight was compared to her.

The pajamas were clean, but the scent of him lingered on the fabric, a subtle blend of his cologne and the familiar essence of the cold, crisp air of a winter's day. The fabric itself, well-worn and carried the weight of countless nights and lazy mornings.

Her clothes had been washed, dried, neatly folded and laid out for her on the couch when she woke up yesterday morning.

She'd thanked Lael for taking the time to launder them, but the woman had denied any involvement which left Liam, Dwight's shy six-year-old or the moody cowboy himself.

It was a thoughtful gesture she'd remember to thank him for. He'd make a grunting sound, mumble something like, "no problem" and that would be the end of it.

But she truly was grateful for all he'd done. She'd never be able to thank him enough for saving their lives or forget how he'd tenderly held her while she'd cried after losing Hogue.

Dwight Murtaugh was a complex man, with a gentle and caring heart that was often overshadowed by his stoic and emotionally distant demeanor.

Every so often, Dwight's prickly nature would rear its head, leaving Anna with a sense of unease. It wasn't that he was unkind or unwelcoming, but there was an underlying tension between the two of them.

She could see him in her mind, taking the same care with her laundry as he had when he'd removed her wet clothing. Those moments when he'd first brought her in from the cold and laid her on the couch were foggy, but she could hear his words clearly, softly guiding her through the steps, making sure she wasn't scared or offended by his careful undertakings.

His hands on her skin had generated the opposite feelings. Sure, knowing her host had seen so much of her body made Anna terribly uncomfortable at times, but she couldn't ignore Dwight's thoughtfulness. Or the effect he had on her.

He was a man of few words, and Lael did her best to make Anna feel at ease. Yet, they both maintained a respectful distance. It was as if, having gone through the pain of losing a daughter and a wife themselves, they understood Anna's withdrawal from human interaction. They seemed to know that she was grieving and needed space to process her feelings, so they gave her room to be alone with her thoughts.

Little Liam, on the other hand, was keeping a steady eye on Anna. He'd occupied a small corner of the living room for most of the day, keeping quietly to himself as he compiled pages of carefully drawn pictures.

He had a mop of dark red hair, and his blue eyes were deep pools of curiosity and innocence. Anna thought he was adorable. Despite his young age, the boy seemed to have an old soul, constantly observing her.

Maybe it was just his childlike innocence shining through, or perhaps it was his unmasked and prideless concern for the strange woman in his house. Whatever it was, it made Anna's heart ache with a longing she hadn't felt in a long time.

In the agonizing months leading up to John's untimely death, their relationship had deteriorated into a broken mess. Her hopes and dreams of starting a family with him were shattered, leaving her heart cold and empty.

But looking at Liam, she found herself imagining what their children might have looked like. Would they have had his dark hair? His deep-set eyes? The thought brought a bitter-sweet smile to her face. For now, she would just enjoy the company of this sweet, observant little boy who was unknowingly filling a void in her heart.

The view from the living room, her spot since breakfast, was heaven. She could see everything, the barns, paddocks, and pastures —horses, cattle and cowboys all with a center view of the Rocky Mountains capped with a layer of fresh snow. As the sun slowly descended, the blue sky transcended into a gentle shade of pink then purple and finally indigo. A large and pristine moon rose into place over the ranch. Against the darkness of dusk, the soft glow of forgotten Christmas lights hung lowly along the edge of the porch.

Anna had her fingers crossed that the Brewster Ranch would have an equally breathtaking view.

She'd always chosen to look on the brighter side of any circumstance, but as her finger's fidgeted with the outer layer of her empty pockets, she began to lose faith in ever laying claim to that piece of Montana ground. After coming out of her sedative induced sleep and realizing the key was gone, she'd covertly looked everywhere for it.

But to no avail.

If it wasn't here, then it must be either somewhere in the truck, submerged in the creek, or buried under heaps of snow along the trail she and Dwight had taken back to the ranch.

She was alone in the fight against Malachi, and she knew he would eventually catch up with her. She had to find that key. It was her only chance of making it out of this nightmare.

The soft clatter of crayons tumbling into a plastic container drew her attention. Liam was tidying up his coloring materials for the night. A thought suddenly struck her - perhaps he had seen or even found the key.

She moved quietly across the hardwood floor, her sock-clad feet making barely any noise. She settled down next to the disorderly heap of artwork that Liam had created, her legs crossed in front of her.

Picking up the topmost sheet, she studied it, sending an appreciative glance in Liam's direction. "These are wonderful, Liam."

A hint of shyness colored his features as he scooted

closer, pointing out one of the stick figures in the picture. "That's Russell."

"Is Russell your friend?" His head bobbed in affirmation.

"And is this you, tossing him the ball?" This time, his nod was more enthusiastic, accompanied by the ghost of a smile. He began rifling through the pile of drawings, extracting one from near the bottom and handing it to her.

The central focus of the drawing was a brightly adorned Christmas tree. At its pinnacle sat an angel, skillfully drawn with red hair and clutching a heart. His tiny finger traced the figure. "That's mommy. She's an angel now."

A wave of sorrow washed over Anna, her heart fracturing at the innocent revelation. The weight of the child's loss hit her hard, reminding her of the immense hole that had been left by her own mother's death. It was a poignant moment, a painful reminder of the fragility of life and the resilience of a child's spirit.

Then, Liam pointed towards the window where she'd been sitting earlier. "That's why daddy hung the Christmas lights. So, she can find us when she looks down from heaven."

From that moment on, Anna knew every twinkling light strung up for the festive season would carry a deeper meaning for her. They were no longer just forgotten holiday decorations, but also lights of love and memories, guiding a lost soul home. Every time she'd see the glow of Christmas lights, she'd think about this moment, about Liam's pure belief, and how a mom's love still lived on in her son's heart.

"Liam." Dwight's deep voice spoke from the doorway. Anna looked up to see a hard glare on his face, a cup in his hand. "Tidy up and wash your hands," he said, sipping the hot contents. "It's almost time for supper."

With his father's instruction, he quickly gathered his box of crayons and stack of artwork and quietly exited the living room.

Anna rose and resumed her place at the window. Dwight followed. Sitting in the opposite matching chair, he rested his sock feet on the stool. "Feeling better?"

His tone was light, almost casual, but Anna could feel the undercurrent of distrust riding along.

"Yes. I am."

"Good, so you won't mind if we talk?" he asked, lifting the cup to his lips.

"That depends on the topic," she answered, honestly.

"Why I had to pull two strangers from a wreck in the middle of a snowstorm." He raised his dark brows. "For starters."

She shot him a weak smile and shrugged her shoulders. "Because I got lost, didn't have snow chains on my tires and the road was ice?"

Dwight stared at her, his eyes raking over her like physical fingers. After a few intense seconds, he put his feet on the floor and sat up. He went back to scrutinizing her with his eyes. "Here's what I know," he said. Reaching into his flannel shirt pocket, he pulled out her driver's license and a single brass key.

Relief flooded Anna. "You found it." She reached for the key, only to have Dwight lay his hand over hers.

"Not until I get some answers."

Her head felt like a tangled ball of yarn, impossible to unravel. She yearned to unload all her secrets onto Dwight, to let him bear the burden with her. Trusting in his warmth and generosity, she craved the comfort that came with baring her soul. But she was being hunted by a cold-hearted killer. It was better that Dwight and Lael stayed in the blissful ignorance of the secret that was Harmony.

The weight of her secrets could bring everything crashing down around them. Telling them the twisted story about Malachi and the horrible truth behind John's death would mean she'd also have to tell them what really happened to Hogue. She couldn't bear that. Plus, everyone she'd shared her secret with was dead.

"Well?" The fiery blue flecks in Dwight's eyes sparked with intensity as they stared at each other in this quiet standoff. The warmth of his palm crept up her arm and through her chest.

Anna weighed the options, knowing that revealing her secrets could put Dwight and his family in danger. But if she stayed silent, there would be no way to earn his trust. In the end, safeguarding their well-being was a small sacrifice to make for them to stay safe.

Soon, the snow would melt, and she'd be on her way.

To where? In what? She didn't have a vehicle or money.

Deciding she'd think about that later, she quickly reverted to her childhood tactics of making up stories. She pulled her hand from under his, having a strange inclination that he might see through the lie she was about to deliver if he was touching her.

"I never really knew Harmony," she started. "The town was a distant memory that my parents abandoned before I was born. But then I got a letter from my grandma, inviting me to stay with her there. Little did I know, she had terminal cancer. She died last fall."

Dwight continued to stare at her as he held up the key. "And this?"

"It's a key to her house. It has sentimental value. That's all."

"Go on," he instructed.

"When she died, my uncle kicked me out." Anna hated lying. It made her feel dirty and manipulative. "Hogue and my grandma were friends and neighbors for years. When he found out I had no place to go, he told me about his ranch."

He raised an eyebrow. "The Brewster place?"

She nodded. "Yes, that's right. Hogue said his brother had recently died, and he wanted to sell it, so we climbed in the truck and headed towards Copper Creek."

"Who shot Hogue?" he asked, his eyes narrowing with suspicion. "The uncle?"

Crap. "Um, no."

"Then who?"

"I don't know. We got lost and then the truck had a flat tire." If only Dwight hadn't found her driver's license, she could have invented a fictional town and last name instead of a place where everyone knew her as Anna Brewster. "He was a stranger who stopped to help."

"Some stranger shot him?"

"Yes." The lies were rolling off her tongue like second nature, but inside she was screaming. She could still feel the weight of the gun in her hand as she fought Malachi for it, the recoil as it fired, and the sickening thud as it hit Hogue. The metallic stench of blood flooded her senses, and she could see vividly the bright red stain that spread across his body as she scrambled to get him into the truck. "The guy wanted my purse, but Hogue refused to let him have it, so he pulled a gun."

Dwight's bottom jaw rolled from side to side. "Did you get a look at this guy?"

Think, Anna! Think! "No. It was getting dark, and he stayed in the shadows."

"Hair color? Height? Weight? Age?" he pressed. "Anything at all to help nail the guy?"

"Ah," she stammered and pretended to remember. "He had a hoodie on, so I couldn't see the color of his hair or guess his age. But he was about your height and weight."

Dwight sat back in the chair, held the cup in both hands as he stared down at it. Then, he began to nod. "Okay."

Her shoulders relaxed. He was buying the lie. Thank God.

Taking his cup with him, he stood. "One more thing."

"Yes?"

"Why not find a place closer to your parents or in Harmony? Why Copper Creek?"

That she could answer truthfully. Hogue's words had set off a firestorm in Anna's young mind, burning bright and wild just like the land he described. Even now, she could practically feel the dirt beneath her feet, smell the sweet hay and hear the cattle lowing. It was all she ever wanted, a place to call home. And with each word, her own yearning had grown stronger, until it consumed her entirely. "It's just the way Hogue talked about the ranch. The way he described the land, the house and his childhood. When I was a little girl, I used to lie in bed thinking about Copper Creek and what it would be like to live there. The Brewster place is a dream come true for me."

Dwight cleared his throat, bent his head and scrubbed a hand over the back of his neck as he stepped to the window. "A dream, huh?"

She felt heat rush to her cheeks. "Yeah, but I guess a man who's lived on a ranch all his life thinks that's silly."

"Nope. Not silly at all." He turned around and took a few steps towards the kitchen, but before striding away, he paused to glance back at her. "But if I were you, I'd come up with a more convincing lie than what you just spouted. The sheriff won't be fooled by that bullshit any more than I am."

Chapter Seven

Dwight leaned against the kitchen counter, his eyes fixed on Anna, who was still perched in the chair at the living room window. He watched her fingers trace invisible lines on the denim of her jeans as she answered Nolan's questions—a map of her worries and fears etched into the fabric of her existence.

After their conversation, Dwight had texted a photo of Anna's driver's license to the sheriff.

He thought maybe if Nolan had this information beforehand, he could dig up something and catch Anna in a lie about what really happened to Hogue. But from what he'd overheard so far, Anna was sticking to her story about a sick grandma and some mysterious stranger.

Dwight's fingers played with the brass key, hidden in the right front pocket of his well-worn jeans. He knew it might unlock Pandora's box, and he wasn't ready to give up his only leverage just yet. Despite his respect for Sheriff Blackfeather, he couldn't risk losing control of whatever situation this was shaping up to be and letting someone else take away his ability to protect Anna.

As Dwight probed her for answers about the key and the man who had shot Hogue, he couldn't help but notice the way her eyes flickered with hidden emotions. They held a certain sparkle that hinted at secrets and buried feelings. But beneath it all, there was a glimmer of fear that she couldn't quite disguise. It pulsed through her, making her stance subtly tense and causing a slight tremor in her voice.

Despite her strength, there was fragility there too, like the delicate lacework of frost on his early morning windows—beautiful but easily shattered with one thoughtless touch.

Her body reacted with a start to the sudden movements, her slender frame tensing up like a startled deer sensing danger. He noted the way her shoulders would hunch, defensively, when voices boomed louder than expected, and how she'd often retreat within herself in an attempt to become smaller, less noticeable, as if she could fade away.

When Dwight looked at her, his eyes would always drift to the area just below her eye, where the skin was an unsettling blend of fading yellows and deepening greens. The bruise marred the softness of Anna's complexion with its jarring discoloration. It was the size and shape of a man's knuckles, not just any man's but those belonging to someone who didn't know how to temper their strength—or their rage.

His jaw clenched harder. It was more than a mere mark; it was a violation of Anna's gentle spirit. He imagined the force behind the blow, could almost hear the sickening thud as flesh struck flesh—imaginary sounds that caused his fists to coil into tight balls of anger and helplessness.

The knowledge that someone could have done such a thing to her, someone she might have once trusted, gnawed at him like a starved animal. He felt something primal stir within him.

Dwight vowed to be more patient and attentive.

Anna may have thought she could hide her true feelings, but he saw right through her front. The fear in her trembling voice and the pain in her haunted eyes revealed everything. She couldn't escape the memory of that dreadful stranger's attack, no matter how hard she tried.

Then came the slip-up, a tiny crack that shattered the perfect lie she thought she'd constructed. She'd accidentally confessed to dreaming about the ranch as a child. As she spoke with that innocent sparkle in her eyes, he'd known at least that part of her story was true.

"Can you describe the man's clothing?" he heard Nolan asked, scribbling down notes on a small pad of paper as Anna answered.

Nolan kept his findings close to the vest, not revealing a thing to Anna or even pushing her for an explanation. And while Dwight was dying for some answers, he was grateful that the sheriff wasn't too tough on her.

Watching Anna's hands twist and turn, he felt his heart clench with a force that was almost painful. He could see her struggling to maintain the lies, but the fear and misery in her eyes tugged at his protective instincts. Every fiber of his being wanted to pull her into his arms and tell her everything was going to be alright.

He forcefully pushed that thought aside, blocking out any thoughts of this woman who stirred forbidden feelings in him.

Anna Sumner was nothing but trouble. He could feel it in his gut and wasn't about to let her get under his skin.

Dwight turned towards the window above the kitchen sink, feeling a heavy weight bear down on him. He squeezed his eyes shut and rubbed at them hard. He should send her packing back to town with Nolan, wash his hands clean of her and this whole damn mess.

But he couldn't. Not yet.

He detested liars, so why was he so drawn to this one? He waited, trusting that Tamara's voice would chime in with a rational answer, but there was only silence. The sound of booted footsteps caused him to look over his shoulder. Nolan re-pocketed the small pad of paper into his jacket pocket, his square chin set hard in thought.

"So?" Dwight asked.

A quick up and down of Nolan's dark brows was followed by a long sigh. "She's lying."

"Tell me something I don't know."

"Well, for starters," Nolan said, lowering his voice so Anna couldn't hear. "She was a foster kid until the Brewster guy and his wife adopted her when she was ten after her parents were killed in a car crash."

Dwight pictured her as a grieving child, much like Liam. Large brown eyes, full of tears, vulnerable and alone and defenseless in a world that showed no mercy to those who needed it most. The idea of innocent Anna Sumner being thrown into the cruel and heartless foster system made bile rise in his throat. But why lie about her relationship to Hogue? Until Dwight knew for sure, he wasn't divulging any information. The key and will would be his and Lael's secret.

But the information Nolan had just sprang on him raised another question. "Is Sumner her married name?" he asked, offering the sheriff a cup of coffee.

"No, though she was engaged." Nolan accepted the cup. "Sumner was her name before she got taken in by the Brewster's. She must've changed it legally right around the time she started gaining traction as a wildlife photographer."

Anna was a wildlife photographer. Dwight couldn't seem to wrap his mind around the woman he knew camping in the wilderness, hidden in some blind, waiting to frame the perfect shot.

It dawned on Dwight that the sheriff had just dumped another fact into his lap. "You said she was engaged."

Nolan sat his cup on the sink and nodded towards the front door. "Walk me out."

Dwight followed him, grabbed his jacket from the hook and stepped onto the porch, a wave of uncertainty clinging to him as he waited for Nolan to explain.

Once the door was closed, he stuffed his hands inside his jacket pockets. "What couldn't you tell me in there?"

Nolan rolled his tongue along the inside of his jaw and shot a hard glance at the window where Anna sat. "Two weeks ago, her fiancé was shot and killed inside his home."

"Damn," Dwight said.

"Yeah," Nolan agreed. "He was a criminal defense lawyer. Everything was torched, including the body and the security footage was wiped clean from the server."

"And?"

"The FBI brought her in for questioning."

"She's a suspect?"

"The only suspect," Nolan clarified.

A criminal defense lawyer was murdered, and the FBI were pointing the finger at his bride to be? "So, there must be incriminating evidence."

"None that I know about." Nolan's brow furrowed as though he couldn't understand why Dwight wasn't automatically condemning Anna for the crime. "She claims there was someone else in the house with them that night and that she's innocent."

"Is that so hard to believe?"

"It is when her description of the guy was, and I quote, "It was dark, he was wearing a hat, and I couldn't see his face." Sound familiar?"

Dwight rubbed his eyes. Her description of the man who'd shot her fiancée was as vague and fabricated as her description of the man who'd shot Hogue. "So, she's bad with details."

Nolan scoffed. "She didn't attend the funeral."

The mention of a funeral took Dwight back to a place and time he wanted to forget but couldn't. He'd had that nightmare a dozen times since Tamara's death and each time the grief that encompassed him took a little more of his soul.

He'd experienced the insurmountable burden a funeral carried with it. The finality of death, the grimness, the somber atmosphere, filled with grief and sorrow, amplifying feelings of sadness and despair.

It had been overwhelming for Lael and Liam. So much so, they'd sat in the truck while Dwight said his goodbyes alone. He'd felt so damn helpless, still did. So, while funerals were intended to provide closure and comfort, they could also serve as painful reminders of the loss and the void left behind. It was a delicate balance between honoring the departed and managing their own grief, making it a challenging and emotionally draining experience some people couldn't handle. But not attending her fiancé's funeral didn't make Anna guilty. "Who was the man she was engaged to?"

"John Tillman, I think, was his name." Nolan turned his back to the window. "She hasn't been seen since she left the police station in Harmony."

"And you think she's running because she's guilty?"

Nolan's left brow rose high on his forehead. "Don't you?"

"I don't know, but if she's telling the truth—"

"Come on..."

"If," Dwight held up a finger to stall the sheriff's denial. "Someone else was in the house and shot Tillman, then she's running for her life, Nolan. Not because she's guilty."

"I read the file, Dwight," Nolan continued. "She was the only one with access to his house and according to friends of the deceased, their relationship was rocky."

Those were hardly compelling points, and Dwight refused to believe she was guilty based on those flimsy facts. Having access to Tillman's house gave her the opportunity, but what motive did she have?

"You saw her face," Dwight said. "Maybe it was self-defense."

"There was no indication in the report that Tillman was violent," Nolan told him. "And don't you think, if it had been self-defense, she would have mentioned it?"

The sheriff had a point, but if Tillman didn't leave the bruise, then who had? There was so much they didn't know. Dwight knew that if the sheriff was convinced Anna was the one who'd killed Tillman, he'd need indisputable proof to change his mind.

Nolan's cell phone buzzed. Retrieving it from his pocket, he looked at the screen and cursed under his breath. "The autopsy on Brewster's been delayed. Damn avalanche."

Dwight hadn't thought about there being an autopsy or how they'd handle Hogue's burial once the body was released.

"Let me know when we can make funeral arrangements," Dwight said, reaching for the doorknob.

"You realize that if the bullet pulled out of Hogue Brewster matches the one in John Tillman, the FBI will be coming for her?"

That fact hadn't escaped Dwight. "How long before you know?"

"The county doesn't have the ballistic equipment to do an accurate analysis, so the bullet will be sent to the feds." Nolan stopped on the edge of the porch, his thumbs hanging loosely in his duty belt. "But, hopefully, the results will be back before you become her next victim."

"Jesus, Nolan."

"You can't deny that men have a way of turning up dead around this woman."

Or Anna had just been in the wrong place at the wrong time when Tillman was shot. But what about Hogue?

Nolan threw up a hand as he headed towards his vehicle. "I'll be in touch. In the meantime, watch your back."

Dwight stepped inside the house, his hands freezing from the cold and his mind reeling with what Nolan had told him.

What if Anna was running for her life? The question was like a warning shot, making Dwight's stomach churn with uneasiness as he thought about the prospect of a new threat that might be headed towards the Sweet Surrender.

He shut the door with a heavy thud and twisted the lock, feeling a twinge of anxiety ripple through him. It wasn't an automatic response, one that came from growing up in a rough neighborhood where locking your doors was second nature.

Dwight couldn't remember the last time he'd use the deadbolt. Living in the small town of Copper Creek, surrounded by never-ending ranches, everything revolved around the land. It was a place where everyone knew each other's business and relied on one another for survival. When times were tough, people had each other's backs, always willing to lend a hand or a shoulder to cry on. Their bonds were unbreakable, forged through years of working the earth side by side. They were more than neighbors, they were family.

But Dwight was a firm believer in cause and effect. Life was a series of calculated moves, each one setting off a chain reaction. Every move Anna made, every decision she took, had consequences that could come crashing down at any moment. John Tillman's murder was just another domino in the chain, hurtling towards her and threatening to bring all her secrets tumbling out.

It was only a matter of time before she had to face what had happened in Harmony, whether it be today, tomorrow, or months from now. As a neighboring ranch owner, Anna's ties to the Brewster ranch placed her and his family in a vulnerable situation.

Dwight knew he needed to uncover who - or what - was following in the wake of the dominoes, but Anna wasn't telling him anything. He'd saved her from the cold waters of the creek, taken her into his home and given her shelter.

But could he convince her that he was an ally, not an enemy?

Chapter Eight

ANNA HAD PROMISED DWIGHT SHE WOULDN'T venture too far from the house and yard. He'd cited the dangers of an old abandoned mine on the property. But she knew it was more than his fear of her stumbling into a pit.

When he left the house this morning for his usual ranch tasks, a gun was holstered at his side. Whatever he and Blackfeather had discussed while on the porch had Dwight taking precautions. Even Lael seemed to be looking over her shoulder but hadn't taken up arms yet.

Ordinarily, her desire for exploration would have tempted her to push that promise to the limit. But she wasn't too keen on pushing the cowboy to his. Since the sheriff's visit, Dwight seemed like a changed man. Less gruff towards her, but more on edge.

Though she was grateful for a warm fire and the safety of the ranch, she needed to fill her lungs with fresh air. Grabbing a heavy-duty jacket Lael had lent her from the hook by the front door, Anna headed outside to take in the beauty of the day.

The ranch was a breathtaking sight after the snow-storm, like something out of a postcard. The fields were blanketed in pure white, the trees glittered with ice crystals, and the air was crisp and still. It was enough to take your breath away and make you believe in magic.

The sun was at its peak, shining fiercely on the snowy mountains. With squinted eyes, she made her way through the yard, towards the gravel road that snaked behind the house and led to the barns and paddocks.

Against the backdrop of the glistening white landscape, the sturdy forms of Black Angus cattle could be seen dotting the fields in the distance, their dark hides contrasting starkly with the snow. Closer to the house, the once pristine ground had been transformed into a patchwork of tracks and trails, evidence of the bustling activity of ranch hands and the rumbling passage of diesel trucks. Footprints and hoof prints crisscrossed the snow, leading from the barn to the fields and back again, while the imprints of tire treads marked the paths where vehicles had plowed through the snow to tend to the livestock and maintain the ranch's operations.

Anna paused at the rough-hewn fence marking the boundary of the pasture, her breath frosting in the cold winter air. She let herself believe that the universe would right itself and justice would prevail. But deep down, she knew the truth. Evil most often won.

Something in the distance caught her attention. A vision of strength and masculinity, Dwight sat tall atop his horse, a dark figure against the snow-covered landscape. The steady clop-clop of the horse's hooves resonated across the peaceful landscape, blending with the gentle crunch of snow underfoot as they headed towards the barn. With each step, the horse's hooves kicked up little puffs of snow, leaving a trail of soft, powdery flakes behind. In this serene setting, the horse and rider moved as one, their movements synchronized with the quiet beauty of the scene unfolding around them.

He sat tall in the saddle, his broad shoulders adorned in his heavy winter jacket. A deluge of memories swept through her, overwhelming and bittersweet. She recalled huddling close to him in the bed of that old truck, seeking refuge from the harsh wash of frigid water. She could still feel his strong arm wrapping around her shivering frame, the heady aroma of leather and pine filling her senses.

As Dwight and the horse drew nearer, she noticed the subtle form of his posture, the way his shoulders relaxed into the familiar tempo of the horse's gait. His gloved hands held the reins with gentle authority, a silent communication between man and animal. His dark hair peeked out from beneath a Stetson, strands dancing in the breeze as he guided the horse.

Watching him stirred something inside Anna. He exuded a primal power, completely at ease in his element. To her, he was the epitome of a real cowboy, irresistible and sexy.

She was itching to grab her camera and capture every moment of him in his element, but it, like most of her worldly belongings, was lost in the fire.

Anna considered herself a self-reliant woman and until recently, felt herself strong enough to endure any circumstance. She'd been a wildlife photographer for nearly twelve years, navigated some of the toughest terrain in North America, spent weeks alone in the wilderness and faced dangerous animals.

She knew how to keep her distance from deadly beasts, but also how to get up close and personal for the perfect shot. It took agility and nerves of steel to handle the heart-pumping moments that turned into life-or-death situations.

Dwight, however, was an entirely different beast. A brooding, enigmatic widower with that gentle touch and sinful good looks. He was the type of man that could break a woman's heart without even trying.

Oh, Anna. There you go letting your imagination run away. Their situation was anything but romantic. It was dangerous and complicated, and she knew Malachi would do whatever it took to get the flash drive which was safely locked away.

But if Malachi got to her before she retrieved it, no one would know the truth about John's death. She'd never be able to prove her innocence.

Anna had lain awake all night thinking about what to do. Hogue was the last of her family and with him gone, there was no one for her to trust except Dwight. He had the key, and he was the only one standing between her and Sheriff Blackfeather.

Dwight went out of sight behind the barn, and Anna shifted her attention back to the house. It wouldn't be long before he came in for supper, giving her an opportunity to speak with him. There was something about Dwight that made her feel at ease, though she couldn't quite put her finger on why. She was grateful for taking that wrong turn and ending up at his doorstep. But as the sun fell over the mountains, he'd still not come in.

Lael didn't seem bothered by his absence, dismissing it as another late night for the rancher. "You get used to it," she told Anna from the kitchen. "My dad was a rancher. Tamara's dad was a rancher and his daddy before him. There's always a fence that needs mending, a tractor that needs fixin' or a sick animal."

At the mention of Tamara, Anna stood up from her chair at the living room window and walked to the kitchen. She leaned a hip against the counter and watched Lael use a rolling pin on the dough she'd just dumped onto the table.

She crossed her arms over her breasts and smiled, wanting to know more about Tamara, but treading softly around Lael's grief. "So, you knew what you were getting into when you married a rancher?"

"Oh, sure I did, and I don't regret a second of my life with Eli Clark. And neither did my daughter. Tamara never complained about Dwight's long hours. In fact, most of the time, she was right beside him doing what needed to be done."

In her mind's eye, Anna could see the vibrant red-haired woman from the photographs, toiling alongside Dwight in the heart of their ranch. She envisioned her with a sun-kissed glow on her freckled skin and her hair under the constraints of a ball cap with some sort of ranch logo stamped across the front.

Dwight, his broad shoulders, handsome face and dirt-covered shirt, next to her. His strong, calloused hands handled the rough ropes and heavy tools with ease. The sweat on his brow would glisten in the midday sun as he worked tirelessly to maintain their way of life.

Lael stopped rolling and shifted to one hip, then pointed a finger in the direction of the barn. "I remember seeing her help him pull a calf from a cow with little Liam strapped to her back in one of those carrier things."

Anna's eyes went wide. "Really?"

Lael, wearing a proud smile, chuckled. "That girl was something."

Anna moved to the table, pulled out a chair and eased into the seat. "What happened to her, Lael?"

Lael pulled open a drawer, retrieved a sturdy metal biscuit cutter, and started punching out dough rounds. "A car wreck," she said simply. "My son Brian and his wife were expecting their first child. Tamara and I put together a baby shower for them at the rec center in town. The storm came in so fast." Lael didn't look up once as she laid the dough on a baking sheet. "She called Dwight to come pick her up in the 4x4, but he was working and missed the call."

Anna's chest tightened. Her heart ached for the cowboy who'd appeared out of nowhere in the blinding blizzard to save her and Hogue, the cruel hands of fate once again dredging up the ghosts of Dwight's past. Anna remembered his face contorted with the agony of that night. The memory of Tamara's wreck flooding back as he tried opening the door.

He'd done for them what he hadn't been able to do for his wife.

"She cut through Shadow Canyon," Lael said, not looking up from her task, each word dropping like a stone in still water. "It snakes through the shadow of two mountains. The sun doesn't reach the payvement enough to melt away the snow and ice. Locals avoid it when it snows, but it's the quickest way in and out of Copper Creek. Her vehicle went off the road near the bridge."

Having been ensnared in the icy grip of a snowstorm, Anna knew the terror of spinning out of control. The violent jolt, the suffocating fear, the uncertain future looming ominously—her life's reel playing out in harrowing slow motion. "I'm so sorry, Lael."

As Lael's hands worked the biscuit dough, deft and practiced, it was almost easy to overlook the tremble that betrayed her buried sorrow. "It was an accident. But Brian blames Dwight. And of course, Dwight blames himself."

Anna knew all too well that guilt and grief were bedfellows. She'd never be able to forgive herself for Hogue's death.

Sniffing, Lael grabbed the baking sheet and slid it

into the preheated oven. "Folks expected Dwight and Tamara to be together forever, and I suppose they will be. He keeps one boot in the grave and the other on the go."

Anna's gaze lingered on Lael, seeing her in a whole new way. Despite the devastating loss of her daughter, this remarkable woman had managed to keep the fabric of life intact for Dwight, Liam, and their entire clan.

"You know," Lael said, taking a wet rag from the sink. "That's where he was the day you and Hogue wrecked. Up on that ridge, mourning my daughter." Her movements were swift as she cleaned the excess flour from the tabletop. "He doesn't want me to know, always making up excuses like replenishing supplies or some other nonsense. But I'm not a fool." Finally, she stopped, braced her hands against the table and bowed her head. "He's grieving himself to death and there's not a damn thing I can do about it."

Sensing Lael was about to lose her composure, Anna reached across the table and took her hand. "He'll get through this and so will you. Brighter days are ahead."

But as she spoke the words, she wondered if Dwight would ever recover from Tamara's death.

Smiling, Lael nodded. "I hope you're right."

Liam burst into the kitchen and climbed into the chair next to Anna. She laughed, thankful for the interruption and rubbed a hand over his hair. "How'd the game go?" she asked, knowing he'd been playing an online video game with his friend Russell.

"I lost," he answered. "Can I have a cookie, grandma?"

"No," Lael said, sternly. "You'll spoil your supper."

"Awe," he protested.

Shoving her bottom lip out, Anna wrapped an arm

around Liam's little shoulders and pleaded, "Come on, grandma. Surely a consolation cookie is in order."

Holding back a grin, Lael grabbed two apples from the basket on the counter. She handed one to Anna and the other to Liam. "Sorry. I'm afraid a consolation apple will have to do."

"Bummer," Anna told Liam and bit in. He giggled and did the same.

After the three of them ate dinner, Anna helped Lael tidy up the kitchen and went back to her spot by the window. Sinking deeper into the comfy chair, Anna's thoughts turned to Tamara. Time hadn't diminished her presence. It lingered within the walls of the home.

It looked as though the woman had just stepped out to run an errand and would return shortly.

In the kitchen, an apron still hung from a hook, lightly stained with remnants of meals Anna knew Tamara had once prepared. A pair of pink snow boots sat by the front door, unused and dusty.

Every corner of the house held remnants of Tamara's presence – her favorite books left untouched on the shelves, her scent lingering on pillows, clothing and fabric.

Dwight couldn't bring himself to let go. He seemed to cling to each item as if it tethered him to the woman he was still very much in love with.

Though life had marched on, and the world outside continued to change, within these walls, time stood still, preserving what looked like a shrine of love and loss.

When bedtime rolled around and Dwight hadn't come in, Anna began pacing the living room. She'd spent all afternoon rehearsing what she wanted to say to him, and they'd be no sleep until she said what was on her mind.

She slipped on the jacket again and headed into the winter night to find Dwight. The crisp air nipped at her cheeks as she made her way through the snowy expanse. The cowboys she'd seen earlier had retired to the bunkhouse and she could hear the jovial commotion of working men blowing off steam.

The ranch took on a whole new persona under the cover of darkness. The pristine white snow glittered like diamonds in the soft moonlight, casting a glow over the sprawling fields and rugged terrain. The familiar sights of the day were transformed into mysterious shadows and sparkling silhouettes.

As Anna ventured towards the barn, a sense of unease began to gnaw at her. She couldn't shake the feeling that unseen eyes were watching her every move.

Dwight was nowhere to be found. This was a bad idea. "Stupid, stupid woman," she chided herself.

Suddenly, a branch cracked in the distance, shattering the silence like a gunshot. The hairs on the back of her neck stood up. The low hoot of an owl echoed through the night, its haunting call seeming to taunt the wind as it swept through the trees. The slightest sound filled Anna with a growing sense of suspicion and fear.

Was she alone out here, or was Malachi waiting to pounce? The darkness seemed to close in around her, the shadows dancing with secrets and whispers of danger lurking just beyond her sight.

<h1 style="text-align:center">Chapter Nine</h1>

ANNA'S FIGHT-OR-FLIGHT MODE KICKED IN AND she began scanning the area for a safe place to hide. The house was too far away, and the inside of the barn was even more ominous looking than the wood line from where the noise had originated.

She could run to the bunkhouse. And say what? She'd heard a noise. Humiliating herself would only make things worse. "Calm down," she whispered, wishing she could slow her racing heart that easily.

Anna hadn't come this far and fought off Malachi Wolfe to shrivel into a frightened ball of nerves. Spinning around, she saw the faint glow of a light in one of the outbuildings near the barn.

Another snap, closer and louder than the last, caused her to jump and set out at a dead run.

Go! Go!

She was nearly at the building when the toe of her right shoe caught on the edge of a frozen set of hoof prints left by a horse. She went down, her face and hands plowing through the cold snow, causing her to let out a shriek.

As if staged, she slid to a stop in front of the building as the door swung open. Dwight stepped out, his large body casting a shadow on the white ground. "Anna?"

"Unfortunately, yes," she said, spitting snow and dirt from her bloody mouth. "It's me, making a grand entrance as usual."

Dwight crouched down beside her, the light at his back hiding his features. He reached out and gently took her by the arms. "What happened? What in the hell are you doing out here?"

Grimacing, she held onto his forearms, feeling the strength and solidity of his muscular arms beneath her fingertips. With each flex of his muscles, she could sense the power contained within. "Looking for you."

He led her inside the building and sat her on a wooden bench, then he dug into his back pocket for a handkerchief, retrieved a rolling stool, and sat down in front of her. "Well," he said, the hint of a warmness playing on his lips. "You found me."

Anna scoffed incredulously as Dwight's rough fingers brushed against her swollen lip, a gesture both surprisingly tender and jarring. The pain that shot through her reminded her of the humiliating home-run dive she'd just taken, and she couldn't help but wince. "I thought I heard a noise from the trees, so I started running."

"What kind of noise?" His smile seemed somewhat genuine, but his sharp gaze had a way of piercing through her. And right now, she felt like he could see clearly to her soul. Maybe he could. Maybe he was one of those gifted people who could read minds and uncover secrets.

If only that were true, she wouldn't have been in this weird predicament of orchestrating a conversation that would leave her even more vulnerable. "A branch breaking, but I'm sure it was an owl or something. Are you busy?" she asked, aware she'd adeptly barged into some sort of workshop.

"No. Why?"

As Anna's eyes adjusted to the dim light of the workshop, she couldn't help but marvel at the intricate leather designs adorning the large worktable spanning the length of the room.

She stood up, suddenly feeling out of place and like an intruder. "I should go."

With a suddenness that caught her off guard, his hand reached out, enveloping her wrist in a light grasp. She felt the warmth of his touch as he guided her back to the bench, his fingers steady and reassuring against her skin.

"Relax," he urged softly, his voice a soothing presence. "Take a deep breath and tell me why you're here." His touch conveyed a sense of calm and understanding, grounding her in the moment and the reason for her unexpected visit.

She took a deep fortifying breath. When she felt more relaxed, she pointed to the saddle hanging on the rack beside them. "Did you do this?"

He nodded. "I took up leatherwork after my wife died. It gave my mind somewhere to go."

After John was killed, there hadn't been time for Anna to think about anything other than running. But the pain was there, hiding —waiting for the right time to hit her.

"May I?" she asked, before taking the liberty of examining his beautifully hand tooled artwork.

He shrugged indifferently. "Be my guest."

The rich aroma of leather hung heavy in the air, mingling with the scent of oils and dyes, creating a heady atmosphere that enveloped her senses. She traced the intricate patterns with a finger, mesmerized by the delicate filigree and bold embossing that brought each piece to life. From finely tooled belts and wallets to ornate saddlebags and holsters, the workshop was a treasure trove of leatherwork. "They're beautiful, Dwight."

"Thanks."

"Was leather work something that was passed down to you, like," she hesitated then smiled. "Drinking coffee or are you a self-taught man?"

He laughed. "No. It was just something I wanted to do, so when I wasn't working, I was in here, teaching myself."

Anna glanced at the small cot near the back of the building and felt a streak of envy. Dwight had poured himself into leatherworks and even slept in a bed that was obviously a size too small for him because he missed his wife and couldn't bare to sleep in an empty bed.

Her relationship with John, however, had been so distant and cold, she hadn't thought twice about sleeping in a bed without him.

Dwight rolled himself over to where she was, rested his elbow on the worktable and gave his jaw a hard scrub. "How did you cope with John's death?"

She winced. So, he did know. "Hogue," she said. "If it hadn't been for him, I would have curled into a ball and given up."

He sat there in quiet reflection, observing her as she struggled to find the words, she needed to explain herself. "I didn't want to lie to you, but..."

"You didn't know if you could trust me?" he replied.

"I guess since you know about John, you know what happened in Harmony."

"I know what the sheriff told me."

"I shot John."

His eyes narrowed. "Is that a confession?"

"Might as well be," she said, wrapping her arms

around her midriff as the feeling of hopelessness re-turned. "The authorities in Harmony were ready to cru-cify me. They were like a pack of wild dogs. All they care about is closing the case. They didn't even listen to what I had to say."

"So, you ran?"

"Not exactly."

"You came here to talk. So talk."

"To be clear," she hesitated, her eyes squeezing shut. She couldn't believe she was about to say this. "I came here to ask you for help."

Surprise registered on his face.

"Look," she continued, sinking back into her seat. "I'm not in the habit of being rescued or asking for help. But that seems to be all I've done since I met you. Hon-estly, though, I'm strong and assertive and—"

"Rambling," he finished, this time revealing a sexy crooked smile that made her lose her breath.

"Usually, no," she said, laughing airily. "But lately..."

"We'll chalk it up to stress," he said, his teasing tone clearly meant to help her relax.

"The truth is, Hogue is gone, and I got nobody left I can trust."

His eyes swirled dark, and his smile faded. "Do you trust me, Anna?"

The question brushed against her like a seductive touch, easily breaking through the fragile barrier of their new friendship.

She swallowed. "With my life."

Slowly, he moved closer. So close, in fact, she could feel the heat of his body radiating through her jeans and jacket. Positioning his elbows on his knees, his eyes re-sumed their drilling technique. "Then no more secrets. I want to know everything."

Anna's mouth went dry, and her scraped palms

turned sweaty. She definitely had to get a handle on her body's response to this man. Not only was he good-looking, but he was also quick on his feet, resourceful and intelligent. It was a dynamic combination to have on one's side. "Okay, but first, I need a ride into town."

"Why?"

"To get the evidence I need to prove I'm innocent."

THE NEXT MORNING, Dwight dragged himself out of bed an hour and a half later than usual, in dire need of a strong cup of Lael's wake-you-or-break-you coffee. He fumbled with the buttons on his blue and white flannel shirt, letting out a low curse when one popped off, bounced down the steps and skidded under the table that sat by the door.

Now that Tamara wasn't there to darn his clothes, he'd taken to buying new ones. But they didn't feel like his. They didn't have Tamara's tender loving care stitched into their mended seams. As a result, he had a closet full of clothes he didn't wear. This shirt was one of his favorites. He'd retrieved it from Tamara's mending basket shortly after her death.

Dwight made a mental note to salvage the button and add it to Tamara's button jar.

As agreed, he was taking Anna into town this morning. For exactly what, he wasn't sure, but maybe he'd finally get some answers. She'd looked relieved when he'd asked about Tillman. It was as if she'd wanted to get her side of the story off her chest.

Like the mornings before, Dwight could hear the women talking as he got closer to the kitchen. The smell of bacon and eggs stirring his empty stomach into a low growl that made him rub his belly. When he rounded the corner and looked up, he was struck by a sight that both warmed his heart and gave him pause.

Anna sat at the kitchen table, sipping on her coffee with a peaceful expression on her face. Her outfit, unmistakably Lael's, was the epitome of comfort and functionality. The broken-in jeans hugged her curves in all the right places, their faded and frayed edges adding a touch of ruggedness to her look. A snug pink sweater enveloped her upper body, its plush knit warding off the morning chill and bringing a rosy flush to her cheeks. She casually pushed up the sleeves, revealing smooth, creamy skin on her forearms.

And there was Lael, chatting away with her like old friends. It was a touching moment, one that highlighted a strange and unexpected sense of hope and happiness into his quiet home.

In that moment, it dawned on him just how forlorn the house had been since Tamara's passing. A weighty sorrow that clung to every nook and cranny, but with Anna's arrival, laughter and light had returned.

The golden beams of morning light filtering through the window cast a gentle glow on Anna's serene features.

The night before, she'd seemed like a completely different person - with bruises and a look of fear in her eyes, unsure of how he would respond to her request for help. But now, as he stood watching her from the doorway, he was struck by her transformation.

Her chestnut tresses cascaded down her back in gentle waves, each strand aglow with a subtle radiance. They framed her features with a natural elegance, highlighting the delicate curve of her jaw and the graceful arch of her neck.

But it was those mesmerizing brown eyes that truly

snagged his attention - their warm depths hinting at both intelligence and a touch of enigma.

As Dwight watched her interact effortlessly with Lael and Liam, he couldn't help but marvel at how quickly she'd become a part of their lives. In just a few short days, she'd brought an undeniable sense of joy and lightness to their household, and even Dwight himself couldn't deny the impact she had made. And it wasn't just him—Lael and Liam seemed happier too, their laughter ringing out more freely than before.

They were only going into town, so the unexpected tug of anticipation rippling through him was surprising. And he had to admit that there was something about Anna, a depth beyond her predicament that intrigued him.

This woman had nothing left, no family, no fiancé. No one she could trust but him. And that caused a nagging sense of trepidation to settle over him.

"Ah-oh," Lael said, pulling him from his reflections. "I know that look."

He leaned a shoulder against the doorframe. "What look?"

"A cranky bear coming out of hibernation," Lael answered, hiding her smirk behind her cup.

Liam snickered and ducked his head.

"I don't know what you're talking about," Dwight said, hiding his fatigue behind a raised eyebrow and a hearty pat to his chest. "I slept like a baby and I'm never cranky."

Lael snorted.

Liam covered his mouth to keep from spewing milk everywhere.

The truth was, Dwight hadn't slept well and if not for their house guest, he would have answered Lael in short grunts instead of attempting humor and politeness. The ambiguous nature of last night's noise from the trees had plagued his rest and rousted him with the slightest sound. He'd practically worn a path from the bed to the window overlooking the barnyard.

Rising from her chair, Anna made her way to the cabinet, retrieving a cup and filling it with coffee before passing it to Dwight with a warm smile gracing her features. "Will this help to soothe the savage beast?"

Normally, no, but Anna had a way of looking at him with those soft brown eyes that melted his resistance and calmed his restless soul. "Thanks," he said, returning her smile as he accepted the cup. "It's a start."

After seeing her safely back to the house, he'd walked the fence that separated the yard from the barn. He hadn't been able to shake the feeling of unease that crept up his spine when she'd mentioned hearing a noise.

Despite her reassurances, he'd needed to make sure there wasn't anyone in the woods. As he'd made his way through the snow, his boots sinking into the undis-turbed fresh powder, he'd noticed something disturbing. Large boot prints, leading towards a juniper tree just within view of the house. Someone had been out there in the woods last night, watching her from afar.

That pissed him off and settled every nerve he had on high alert. He'd check with his men to make sure none of them had been out there before silently sounding the alarm.

"Save any o' them eggs for me?" he drawled, ruffling Liam's hair as he slid into a chair beside his son.

Mouth full, the boy mumbled, "Grandma saved you some."

Lael rose from the table, gesturing for Dwight to take the seat. "I'll get you a plate."

He took a long sip of coffee, savoring the rich flavor.

Anna sat across from him, her demeanor more relaxed than he had seen before. Even with the bruises on her lip, she still had a glow about her. "How'd you sleep?"

She smiled. "Better than I have in a while."

Dwight guessed that was because of their talk. Having someone else to share the burden of a murder charge had to have an intense emotional impact on a person.

Lael sat his plate on the table in front of him. "Anna told me you two were going into town this morning."

He forked a helping of eggs and raised them to his mouth. "Sonny will be close by if you need him."

Tossing a dishrag over her shoulder, she cast him a lingering glance, opting to let his comment slide. Dwight and Lael had developed a silent understanding over time, a form of communication that spoke volumes without the need for words. Their bond resembled that of couples who'd grown accustomed to each other's unspoken cues, a connection that had evolved in the wake of Tamara's death. She'd made a mental note, he could see it in her eyes, to heed his warning and save her questions for a time when Anna wasn't present. He'd tell her about the watcher in the woods, but not now.

"Would you mind picking up some supplies before you head back?' Lael asked, filling the sink with water intent on doing the morning dishes.

"I don't mind, but she's leading this expedition," he said, looking up from his plate at Anna.

"Oh," she answered, surprised that the choice of whether they could pick up Lael's supplies had been left to her. "Yes. We can do that. I'm just stopping by the post office."

Could it be? The brass key in his pocket opened a PO box. If so, it was a clever, covert and safe way to keep something a secret. What was in the box? Who'd sent it? Was it something that could convict or clear Anna?

"Text me a list." He bit a strip of bacon in half.

"You don't need a list," Lael told him. "Baxter's has finally modernized their shopping experience and added an online app. I put in an order this morning."

Excitement wasn't a common visitor in Dwight's life these days, but there it was, bubbling up in his chest—the eager anticipation of uncovering the contents of that post office box.

Lael deposited Liam's empty plate into the sink. "Come on. Let's get you dressed."

The atmosphere in the kitchen fell deftly silent after that and an odd tension settled between Dwight and Anna.

"I'm going to need that key back," she told him, sipping her coffee.

Taking a bite of his toast, he glanced at her with a look that answered for him.

"What?" she asked. "Think I'm going to run away once I have it?"

Dwight shrugged his shoulder. "Maybe."

"Not likely," she replied. "Like you said, my truck is at the bottom of the creek, and I can't ride a horse worth a damn."

"Ah. I see." He narrowed his eyes in an accusing, yet playful manner. "So, you were pretending to be asleep the first time the sheriff was here?"

She winced. "Ugh, he's a real hardass, ain't he?"

"He's just doing his job," Dwight replied carefully, acknowledging the seriousness of the situation without sugarcoating it. He held back from revealing the sheriff's full disdain, opting instead for a measured response. "But compared to the FBI, Nolan's a teddy bear."

Her face paled and he saw her swallow. "FBI?"

"They're analyzing bullet as we speak, Anna."

She sank back in the chair.

Dwight wanted to believe she was innocent in both deaths. The crushed expression on her face made him question everything.

"But if you're innocent, then you have nothing to worry about. Right?"

She didn't answer. She sat unmoved, frozen and staring into space. Her mien had gone from bright and optimistic to condemned and lost again.

And he'd instigated the change.

Sighing, he stretched a leg out, dug into his pocket and pulled out the key. He laid it on the table, the clinking sound snapping her out of the zombie-like state.

"Don't make me regret this."

She picked it up and curled her fingers around it. "I won't, Dwight. Whatever happens, I'm done running."

"We should get going." He pushed his plate back and rose.

He and Anna were on their way to town within a few minutes. It was a quiet ride. It seemed neither of them felt the need to fill the time with idle chit-chat. The main highway was mostly clear of snow. Traffic was flowing in and out of town in the usual manner.

After a quick stop at Baxter's Grocery to pick up Lael's order, Dwight guided the truck into an empty parking space in front of the post office and shut the engine off.

He couldn't put his finger on it, but there was something about Anna that made him trust her not to run now that she had that key. She had a look in her eyes, like she'd been through hell and back, and all she wanted now was some kind of peace.

Though she hadn't divulged everything to him yet,

he knew someone was after her and he wasn't leaving her unguarded for a second.

He stepped out of the truck and joined her on the sidewalk. Copper Creek was what some would call a one-horse town - population less than a thousand - and Dwight knew nearly every person by name. It gave him some sense of security, knowing he could protect her better here than anywhere else. But it also meant that everyone knew his story, and they couldn't help but stare as he walked with Anna by his side.

He had made a promise to never love another woman after Tamara and he intended to keep that promise till the day he died. But these people didn't know the truth behind his stoic facade.

He was thankful for that.

Dwight never cared much about what others thought of him, but their judgmental looks only added to the guilt he carried whenever he was around Anna.

His only concern right now was making sure she was safe. Gently taking her elbow, he led her towards the front door of the post office. Her eyes anxiously darted around the area, taking in the risks and escape routes in the event the situation turned threatening. They'd nearly made it up the steps when he saw Brian Clark walking towards the front door.

Dread rippled through Dwight. *Not now. Please, just keep walking.*

If he'd been alone, he'd have quickly turned and gone the other way, but he wasn't. And there wasn't time to explain family dynamics to Anna, so he braced himself.

Brian glanced up, doing a double take as he exited the building. His eyes bounced from Dwight to Anna and then back to Dwight. Distain clouded his features, distinct Clark family characteristics he'd once shared with Tamara.

With a wary eye, Dwight took point in front of Anna, steeling himself for Brian's inevitable verbal attack. He was careful not to make too obvious of a move, wanting to protect her without causing any unnecessary commotion. He held the door open for her, masking his protective act with a seamless display of chivalry. All the while, keeping an ever-watchful eye on the brewing storm that was Brian.

"Dwight," Brian gave a one word greeting.

"Brian," he answered back.

Brian's jaw muscles tightened as his hooded eyes took in Anna from head to toe. "New friend?"

"New neighbor," Dwight clarified. "That's all."

"I'm sure," Brian scoffed.

"Um, hi," Anna greeted him with a smile and the offering of a handshake. "I'm Anna Brewster. Ronnie's niece."

Brian grunted, his hate-filled eyes digging into Anna.

"This is Brian Clark," Dwight supplied. "My brother-in-law."

"Ex-brother-in-law," Brian bit out. "My sister is dead, remember?"

Dwight was tired of standing by in quiet repose, letting a grief-filled man he'd once thought of as the brother he never had, rake him over the coals. "I wasn't the one who let her drive home that night," he seethed. "You were."

Brian's brown eyes blazed with self-loathing and anger. "Go to hell."

Dwight stepped closer until he was nearly nose-to-nose with the man. "I'm already there and every goddamn day I wake up without my wife, I'm reminded of it."

Chapter Ten

ANNA DID HER BEST TO STAY FOCUSED AS SHE and Dwight weaved through the crowded post office, her mind set on finding the box.

After all, inside it was the crucial piece of damning evidence that would help clear her name and put Malachi behind bars. But she couldn't shake off what had just transpired.

Brian's words lingered, accusing Dwight of Tamara's death. The blame game weighed heavily on Dwight's shoulders.

"Are you okay?" she asked, her voice hushed amid the wandering eyes of people who'd just witnessed the confrontation at the front door.

"I'm fine," Dwight returned, his features a combination of anger, grief and weariness. "Let's just find the box and get the hell out of here. What number is it?"

"628."

Silently counting the boxes, they scanned the numbers.

"Found it," he declared with a hint of relief in his voice.

With trembling hands, Anna inserted the key into the lock and turned it. She gingerly pushed open the door, her heart racing with anticipation. The box inside held her last chance at a fresh start. Furtively glancing over her shoulder, she reached for the large manilla envelope and pulled it out of the box.

Placing a hand on her lower back, he turned her towards the door. They hurried to the truck and climbed in. He backed out of the parking space and set a course for the ranch.

"Something is off," she said, her fingers feeling the envelope.

He frowned. "What do you mean, off?"

After tearing open the seal, Anna swiftly emptied the contents into her lap, her reaction a mix of shock and disbelief. "Oh, my god."

Dwight, visibly stunned by the sight, let out a low whistle. "That's a lot of cash," he remarked, his tone reflecting the gravity of the situation.

She made a quick estimate, realizing that the pile of money had to be in the thousands of dollars.

"That's your proof?" he asked, his incredulity evident.

"No." Shaking her head, she sifted through the stacks of money until she unearthed a protective case housing a memory card she'd taken from her camera moments before John was shot. Holding it up for Dwight to see, she declared, "This is. Hogue mailed it to Ronnie's PO Box before we left Colorado."

"So, that's starting over money," he said.

"Yeah. I guess so." As tears welled up in her eyes, Anna, overwhelmed by a flood of emotions, murmured, "It must be his entire life savings."

Again, guilt and grief washed over Anna, and she couldn't hold back the tears. The selflessness of Hogue's generosity and what she'd done to him broke her. "I don't deserve this."

Dwight reached over, his large hand engulfing hers as he gave it a gentle squeeze. "Love isn't about what we deserve. It's about what we give freely, without expectations, Anna."

She felt the timbre of his voice settle over her like the warmth of a sunset, soothing and rich. It was as if every syllable he spoke carried its own weight and left an imprint on her heart. The way he said her name, elongating the vowels just so, made her heart flutter a bit.

His eyes were such an intriguing shade of blue and they held hers with such fierce certainty that she found herself lost in them, adrift in their depths.

She realized then just how lucky Tamara had been to have this man for a husband. John had never spoken anything so meaningful, poetic or touching as what Dwight had just said.

Dwight's expression turned remorseful. "I should have told you this before. There was a will inside Hogue's wallet. He left you the ranch and the store in Harmony. You have it all."

But she didn't. Her all was gone. Her family and fiancé were dead. John and Hogue had lost their life because of her and now, she was alone.

That horrible sense of loss she'd felt when her parents died invaded her once again, ripping away that small glimmer of hope she'd been holding onto. She felt too numb to speak. Laying her head against the window, she closed her eyes.

As they drove closer to the Sweet Surrender, the loss deepened. She had to get away from Dwight and his family. It was time she struck out on her own and faced whatever was to come by herself.

The threat of losing someone else she cared about was simply too much. If Lael, Liam or Dwight got in the way, Malachi wouldn't hesitate to hurt them to get the memory card.

Anna raised her head, smeared away the dampness from her eyes and began stuffing the cash back into the envelope. "Take me to the Brewster ranch."

"That's not a good idea," he said, his eyes darting from the road to her as he spoke. "The house...it's not what you think it is. It needs work, Anna.

"I have money," she told him. "I'll hire someone to do repairs."

"Anna—"

"Dwight! Please! Just take me there!"

As the truck lumbered to a stop, he steered it onto the shoulder. This was the spot in the road where she'd taken that fateful wrong turn during the blizzard, just one of many times she'd lost her way and found herself in dire circumstances. After a few moments of silence, she heard him take a deep breath and let it out slowly. "No."

Overwhelmed, she gathered the envelope in her arm and grabbed hold of the door latch. "Then I'll walk."

But before she could get out, Dwight's big hand closed around her arm. "Don't."

His tender command hit the already bruised areas of her heart. "Please," she begged. "Just let me go."

Dwight recoiled, his face contorted in agony as if he had been stabbed with a rusty blade, the pain radiating through every fiber of his being. His hold loosened and his chiseled features twisted with fury, revealing a side of him she'd never seen before. "Fine," he said, roughly shifting the truck into gear as he stomped on the gas. "You want to go to the ranch? I'll take you to the ranch."

He drove straight a few miles then turned right onto a rutted-out gravel road. The holes were so big the truck mimicked a ship on a stormy sea, dipping left then right, only to repeat the nauseating process again and again.

Anna clutched the dash as Dwight skillfully maneuvered the rough terrain. Finally, as they rounded a bend in the road, the ranch house came into sight.

"There it is," he sneered. "The Brewster ranch in all its glory, ready and waiting for you to move in."

The old ranch house loomed before her, its dilapidated state washing her in a wave of despair. She could see where the roof had caved in, leaving a gaping hole and exposing the interior to the elements. The front porch was sagging, and every window was either shattered or boarded up. A rusty swing set sat abandoned in the overgrown yard. "But he said..." She paused to swallow the lump in her throat. "He said it was beautiful."

"He lied," Dwight said flatly, his tone emulating his sudden sour mood. "Seen enough?"

Without waiting for her reply, he shifted the truck into reverse and headed back down the drive.

Anna felt so heartbroken. The lovely home she'd dreamed about since she was a little girl was nothing more than a dilapidated shell.

She felt like curling into a ball and giving up. It was one blow after another, and it seemed life was gearing up for a grand slam. She'd always been a fighter, but she wasn't sure she could make it through what was to come. Even with the evidence, there was no sure way to know what would happen once she turned it over to the authorities.

As they passed the wreckage of Hogue's truck, lying turned on its side by the power of the water, she covered her face with her hands and let out a blood curdling scream.

Curling her fingers into fists, she began pounding

the top of the dash. She barely noticed that they'd arrived back at the Sweet Surrender, that the truck had stopped or that Dwight had gotten out and was now standing at her side. "Anna," he said, calmly as he grabbed hold of her arms. "Stop before you hurt yourself."

Her hands throbbed and her insides felt like a bomb had gone off. But slamming her fists into the hard plastic of the dash gave her a physical release that felt so good. She was tired of holding it all in. "I have nothing left!" she screamed through tears. "Everything- everyone I love is gone!"

His arms closed around her, wrangling her rage until it was no more. When she didn't have the strength to fight anymore, she collapsed against him. He cradled the back of her head in his hand as he whispered against her ear. "That's not true," his voice was soft and low. "I'm here and everything is going to be alright."

Anna clung to him, her fingers clutching his jacket like they had the night he'd rescued her. When her tears had ceased, she raised her head and locked eyes with him, instantly feeling a jolt of electricity course through her body. His stunning features softened into a look of intense compassion and warmth that stirred her soul. But it wasn't just his handsome exterior that had her heart racing; there was an undeniable air of self-assuredness and reassurance emanating from him, giving her a sense of safety and stability.

Her eyes hungrily roamed his chiseled features, taking in the perfection of his jawline and the tempting curve of his cheekbone. She yearned to run her fingers through the hair at his collar, longing for the roughness of his beard against her skin as she devoured him with kisses.

And why not? If life had taught her one thing it was

that it was too short to have regrets. She had a chance to kiss Dwight Murtaugh and she was going to take it.

Anna threw caution to the wind and gave in to her desires. Her breath hitched as she reached up, fingers trembling like aspen leaves in a summer storm, finally grazing the dark strands at his nape. Silky soft.

Dwight's eyes, deep and fathomless as a midnight sky, held a spark of curiosity that ignited her boldness. She heard him pull in a sharp startled breath and felt his body stiffen. His lips were warm and patient against hers, but reserved in a way that told her he wasn't giving into the moment.

What did you think? That a simple kiss could make him forget all he's lost? Disappointed and embarrassed, she pulled back. "Sorry. I don't know what came over me."

"It's been a tough day," he said, an unreadable expression clinging to his face.

She touched her fingertip to her lips, the remnants of their kiss lingering sweet. "Nevertheless. I feel very foolish right now."

"Don't," he said, urging her out of the truck. "Let's go inside. You'll feel better once you've had time to wrap your mind around all of this."

She doubted that.

With his arms supporting her, they made their way into the house. It was quiet and still, a tell-tell sign Lael and Liam weren't there. It smelled of chocolate and strongly brewed coffee.

It smelled like home, Anna thought as Dwight carefully removed her jacket and hung it up. He guided her into the kitchen and sat her down at the table. "Lael made brownies before she left," he said, as he proceeded to make a fresh pot of coffee. "Want one?"

She placed her elbows on the table and rested her head in her hands. "No, thanks."

The coffee pot gurgled, and Dwight presented two steaming cups, sliding one in front of her with a smirk. "Here. This'll put hair on your chest."

Anna couldn't help but grin as she lifted her head to look at him. "Great, just what I needed. A hairy chest to deal with."

He let out a deep chuckle, the sound smooth and husky like a caress against her skin. "It's an old saying from my granddad. But it made me a coffee addict by the time I hit double digits."

She took a cautious sip, savoring the rich flavor as she asked, "Did it work?"

Dwight tugged at the front of his flannel shirt, glancing down with a thoughtful yet mischievous expression. "Somethin' did."

She should've let it be what it was. A joke to help improve her mood. But her mind, led by her body's yearnings, meandered down the path of imagination. She could see the expanse of his broad chest muscles covered in a dusting of dark hair, feel the silky texture of it as it grazed against her palm. Oh, what a lovely trip that would be.

"You sure you don't want a brownie?" he asked, clearing his throat. He scooted the plate piled high with the finger food dusted with dark cocoa in front of her.

Anna hadn't the slightest inclination towards the sweet treat, but she took one anyway. "If I must," she said, her eyes dropping to the missing button near the top of his stomach. Placing the brownie back on the plate, she pointed to his shirt. "You lost something."

He looked down. "Yeah," he mused, begrudgingly. "The damn thing rolled under the table this morning as I was coming downstairs."

She sat up straight, happy she could be of some use. "I can sew it back."

"What?" he asked, surprise jerking his brows high as he shielded the missing button with his hand. "No. I mean. It's an old shirt. I'll probably just chuck it into the rag box."

"Really?" she questioned, confounded by his refusal to let her do a simple mend. "It looks fairly new."

"Nope," he replied with a casual smile. "I've had it for years."

Holy cow. He was really protective of that shirt. She shrugged and reclaimed her brownie. "Okay then."

Anna may have made the first move, but Dwight hadn't made a counter motion. End of story. He wasn't interested in finding out what could have been because he was still clinging to his deceased wife.

That should have been reason enough to let whatever was happening between them go. But for her, it wasn't.

Sometimes when their eyes met, the fiery sparks of attraction were impossible to hide. Maybe it was the adrenaline rush of danger or the shared understanding of profound loss that drew them together.

Whatever the reason for the pull between herself and Dwight, had her craving more. She wanted her friendship with him to take root and evolve. She was tired of being lonely, tired of being without what he'd just given her, compassion, empathy, a caring touch and two strong arms holding her tight. Against a world that seemed destined to take everything from her, he'd been there to give her something back.

She wanted more of him and that feeling of contentment only he could give.

But the man's heart was buried deep behind an impenetrable door, guarded by grief and pain. Those were bitter forces she knew well.

Dwight seemed all too eager to surrender to them and live the rest of his life alone. Could she save him from that? Could she make him see that they stood a chance at love and a lasting relationship? If so, how?

"I upheld my part of our deal." He reached for the envelope containing the money and memory card. "It's your turn."

"I'll need a computer," she said, hearing the rumbling of Lael's side-by-side roll up the drive.

He handed her the envelope for safe keeping. "There's one in my workshop. We can meet there after supper. In the meantime, let's keep this between us."

Chapter Eleven

Dwight knelt by the fireplace and began neatly stacking the wood into the metal rack. From the corner of his eye, he could see Anna and Lael as they darted about the kitchen preparing food.

Losing his temper wasn't something he did often and the fact that he'd lost it with Anna made him feel like a bastard.

She'd been moved to tears by the money Hogue had left her and understandably upset by the disrepair of the old Brewster home.

And he'd been an asshole to her all because she'd told him to let her go. He knew he needed to apologize, but if he did, she might want an explanation as to what had set him off.

And that was? My deceased wife tells me I should do the same with her?

He dusted his leather-clad gloves and stood up, feeling like an insanity plea might be his best bet with making things right with Anna.

But crazy or not, apologizing was something he had to do.

Tonight, he decided. When Anna came to his workshop, he'd deliver a heartfelt apology for the jackass he'd been today.

And that kiss she'd planted on him?

He'd forget about it.

Yeah, right. Her lips softly planted against his, eagerly wanting more was all he could think about.

Hanging his jacket and hat by the door, he went to wash up before supper. A delicious spread of pot roast, mashed potatoes and gravy was sitting on the table when he walked into the kitchen and sat down to eat.

Anna had swapped her pullover and denim for a grey sweatsuit that subtly accentuated her womanly curves. Seated opposite him, her features were clearly visible to Dwight. And though he wasn't opposed to enjoying the view, it did present certain concentration issues for him.

Lael had called him out for not paying attention to the conversation. He'd slyly passed it off by grinning and stating that he wasn't into the latest fashion trends of female country music singers.

Returning to his ample serving of pot roast, he managed to steal subtle glances at Anna from the other side of the table while listening for Lael.

Anna had somewhat succeeded in taming her abundant locks into a pile atop her crown. The mass wobbled from left to right as she chuckled at Liam's antics of sculpting a mountain out of mashed potatoes. Loose tendrils of hair had slipped out of place, draping in a disorderly veil down the back of her neck.

Messy seemed to be her signature look. She'd flipped the script on Dwight's definition of disheveled and made it her own. Unlike those uptight women who obsess over every strand of hair and perfectly painted face, she embraced imperfection. Not that he'd ever seen her with a hint of makeup on her flawless skin. From the moment he rescued her from that creek, she had been completely natural and radiant.

At times, when she looked at him, like really looked at him, he felt as if a fragment of himself was slipping away. The sensation was scary as hell.

And her smile.

Damn.

Dwight's heart stuttered like a pickup on a cold morning. She had that effect on him. When Anna smiled at him, heat bloomed in his chest, and he felt alive for the first time in years.

He settled back into his chair, the wood groaning softly under his solid frame. The dining room around him was aglow with the soft golden light from the wrought-iron chandelier overhead, casting an amber hue over the dark wood furnishings and Navajo-inspired décor. This was supposed to be a place of comfort, a sanctuary within their home where he and Tamara shared meals and laughter after long days tending to the land they both loved.

But now, he was entertaining thoughts about another woman, even though he considered himself steadfastly loyal to Tamara.

His palm brushed against the warm ceramic of the serving bowl as he scooped out a hearty pile of fluffy, butter-drenched mashed potatoes. He was struggling with an unsettling disloyalty, like a thistle hitching a ride on his boot—unseen but sharply present. Dwight had always considered himself a man of honor; his word was as strong as the oak fence posts lining their property. But now that foundation seemed to quake beneath him.

Maybe all these burgeoning sensations and emotions he was experiencing could be explained rationally.

Maybe he'd been living in death's somber shadow for so long that he'd forgotten how to feel anything else.

He held on to that, manifesting it into the most logical conclusion. Relieved he'd justified his reasons and realigned his heart and mind, he took another bread roll from the basket and sank his teeth into its soft, warm crust.

Supper was pleasant, but he couldn't shake off the feeling that something in his universe had subtly shifted. It was as though reality, as he understood it, had been gently skewed. The once clear demarcation between safeguarding Anna and maintaining a safe distance had now become indistinct.

There went his living-in-the-shadow-of-death theory.

"What the hell is wrong with you?" he mumbled to himself and tossed down the last of his whiskey before heading towards the front door.

Sliding his arms into the confines of his jacket, he unlocked the deadbolt and ventured into the frosty night without a sound. He stopped at the edge of the porch and took a deep breath, trying to clear his head.

But it was no use. He still felt woozy and a little lightheaded. He couldn't blame it on the whiskey. He had a strong constitution. Maybe he was coming down with the flu or maybe he was just tired. Maybe he needed a shrink or a shaman. "Or a good swift kick in the ass."

Dwight descended the wooden steps, his boots crunching on the snow-covered path leading to his workshop. He had to stay focused on the issue at hand. Keeping Anna safe until whatever she had on that memory card proved her innocence of murder was his top priority.

And then what? Would she take up stakes at the

Brewster ranch now that she knew the state of the house, or would she leave Copper Creek all together?

Anna had a career, a successful one according to the online investigation he'd done. Of course, she'd leave town and that, he decided, was for the best.

The floodlight perched beside the barn bathed the backyard in a soft, white glow. Carl Richardson's silhouette was outlined against the fence, a rifle resting nonchalantly over his shoulder. As he noticed Dwight's approach, he acknowledged him with a nod and ambled towards him. "Evenin', Boss."

"Carl," he responded curtly, shoving his hands into the warm confines of his jacket pockets. "How is everything?"

Carl gave a noncommittal shrug as his gaze roamed over their surroundings. "Quiet so far."

"Let's hope it stays that way," Dwight muttered under his breath, hoping that things would continue to go smoothly. He turned and headed back towards the workshop when he heard the front door creak open and shut, breaking the stillness of the surroundings.

"Wait up," Anna's voice rang out through the night air as she hurried to catch up with him.

Carl cleared his throat, an amused smirk playing on his lips. "You two planning some late-night tooling?"

The leather tooling question was loaded with an innuendo that Dwight didn't appreciate. "That's enough," he told Carl.

With a cocky tilt of his head, Carl flashed a sly grin, adjusted his hat in acknowledgment, and turned to resume his guarding duties.

Dwight's lips tightened as he noted to squash that damn piece of gossip before it spread like wildfire and grew into something that would make things even more awkward between himself and Anna.

"Trouble?" she asked, watching Carl as he walked away.

He noticed the subtle shift in her expression, the way her gaze danced nervously around before landing back on him. Beneath the surface, he sensed a flicker of fear and uncertainty that tugged at his protective instincts. "Don't worry," he said, his voice steady and reassuring. He moved closer, reaching out to take her elbow. "I found tracks near the wood line, so we're keeping a sharp eye out."

"What kind of tracks?"

The most dangerous kind. "Cougar," he lied.

"Seriously?" she exclaimed.

"There's a canyon not far from here," he explained, steering her towards the workshop. "They den there every year, but like I said. There's nothing to worry about."

"I'm not worried," she retorted matter-of-factly. "I just regret not having my camera with me."

They reached the workshop. Chuckling, he opened the door and stepped to the side to let her enter first. "You're the only woman I know who gets elated when she finds out there might be a wild animal stalking the backyard."

"Well," she smiled saucily. "I'm not your average woman."

Her sudden grin caught him off guard, the warm sensation settling just beneath his ribcage. Her throaty chuckle filled the room and was followed by a flirtatious wink that inked lower in his abdomen.

Adjusting his posture, he shrugged off his jacket, casually draping it over a bench, choosing to ignore her remark. "Listen," he said, rubbing his palms together to ward off the cold. "About what happened earlier today."

"I apologized. Can't we just forget about it?"

"This isn't about the kiss, Anna." He clamped a hand around the back of his neck. "It's about me losing my temper at the Brewster place."

"Oh, that," she said, shrugging her shoulders. "It was nothing."

"But I shouldn't have done it."

"Hey," she said. "If you can dismiss me throwing myself at you, I can dismiss you being a little peeved."

He frowned. This wasn't going the way he'd thought it would. "You aren't curious as to why I lost my temper?"

"Maybe." She made a small measurement using her finger and thumb. "Just a little, but then I could ask you the same thing about that kiss."

He'd thought her motives for kissing him were plain as day. She was attracted to him. But was she implying there was something more? And did he have the nerve to delve into those deeper motivations?

Hell, no.

"When you told me to let you go, I just kind of lost it."

"Why?" she asked, her confusion obvious.

Scratching his jaw, he pushed back the leather belt he'd been working on and took a seat on the table, realizing he might have unnecessarily started a conversation that could go south quickly. "Because that's what Tamara tells me to do every day. "Let me go, Dwight.""

Anna bit her bottom lip as compassion filled her eyes. "Oh. I see."

Dwight felt like a fool. "You think I've lost it, don't you?"

"No," she was quick to say. "Not at all."

"It's okay." He sighed. "There's a good chance you might be right."

She reached over and cupped his jaw. It was a gesture

that was comforting and arousing. "I can still hear my mother's voice and before leaving Harmony, I thought I saw John."

Dwight was thankful there were no ghostly apparitions of Tamara haunting him.

"A counselor once told me seeing or hearing lost loved ones was a part of the bereavement process. It's natural. It gives us comfort, so don't feel like you're alone. It's your mind's way of helping you through the process of letting go."

That last comment didn't sit well with him. He didn't want to let go of Tamara. He didn't want there to be a time when he didn't hear her, but maybe that time had already come. And he just hadn't accepted it.

"Dwight?"

Hearing Anna say his name caused him to look up. "Yeah?"

She smiled. "I asked you if there was a password on your laptop?"

"Oh, um, no," he stammered. "Did you bring the card?"

"Yes," she said, reaching into her jacket pocket for the card before tossing her jacket on top of his.

"The computer is over there," he said, pointing to the small desk and the laptop he used for bookkeeping and ordering supplies.

"I normally upload everything to Cloud storage." She popped open the case and gave him a nervous glance. "But there wasn't time. Sending memory cards by mail can be risky. All those security scanners can corrupt the files, but Blake, a photographer friend of mine, designed a protective case. Time to see if his gadget worked."

Dwight spun an office chair around, its caster wheels clinking against the bare concrete floor, and motioned for her to sit.

Once she had, she ran a fingertip across the touch-pad, stirring the computer from its slumber. The screen transitioned from an inky black to the vibrant webpage Dwight had inadvertently left open the previous day.

"Ah, what's this?' she teased.

The image showcased her keen eye for detail and patience for capturing a moment that was both intimate and untamed.

The subject of the photo was a black bear mother. The bear's fur was a deep, rich black when seen from afar. But a closer look revealed a mesmerizing blend of hues, from warm chocolate to smoky charcoal.

At her side, two playful cubs tumbled and frolicked. Their soft fur was ruffled and unkempt from play, making them look more like mischievous balls of fluff than future rulers of the wild.

Momma bear exuded an air of strength and protec-tiveness as she watched her babies, her eyes reflecting a love Dwight had never seen in pictures.

Anna had captured this moment from a daring van-tage point that made Dwight admire her and worry about the dangers of her profession. The photo was au-thentic and unbridled, just like Anna herself — fearless, wild, and breathtakingly beautiful.

She was able to capture the raw essence of nature, its beauty and its untamed grace. As he studied the image, he felt a kinship with bears and the woman who had immortalized them. It was clear that Anna had a deep understanding and respect for this world, and he couldn't help but be drawn in by her talent and passion.

Dwight picked up a straight back chair and sat down beside the desk, knowing there was no way he could backtrack his way out of this. "I was curious about your work."

Her eyes softened as her gaze roamed over his face. "And...?"

He crossed an ankle over his knee and leaned back. "You're very talented."

A warm smile of appreciation spread across her lips. "Yeah?"

"I'm sure I'm not the first person to sing your praises," he said, struck by her humbleness. "You have to know you're good at your job."

"I do and you're not." Still holding that smile, she opened the case housing the memory card and adapter. "But having you sing my praises feels good."

And why was that? He was no photography expert.

She slid the adapter into the port on the side of the laptop and assumed a bleak stare at the screen. "And being good at my job is what got me in this mess."

Dwight frowned, the abrupt change in her attitude drawing him closer. "How so?"

She fidgeted in her seat, her knees tightly pressed together, and her hands clenched between her thighs. "John and I were very independent individuals, married to our careers before we were ever engaged. We'd go days without seeing each other, lost in the demands of our work. When he was on a case, he'd hole up in his office, surviving off greasy takeout meals. And when I was on assignment, I'd often be away for weeks at a time. Our home would become a trail of empty pizza boxes and fast-food wrappers."

Anna hesitated, her eyes flickering with a mix of emotions that Dwight couldn't quite decipher. She took a deep breath, the words spilling out in a rush. "But that's just how we operated - two lone wolves thriving in our own separate worlds."

Dwight sat back in the chair and crossed his arms over his chest, his immediate thought being, why bother to have a relationship at all?

Once he and Tamara had fallen in love, he hadn't wasted a second. He'd been consumed by the desire to spend every waking moment with her, so he proposed with an intensity and urgency that came from the depths of his soul.

Their love was ablaze, consuming them both in a fiery passion. Back then, he couldn't imagine a single day without her by his side. She'd been his everything, and he'd wanted to spend every moment cherishing her. She'd felt the same about him. But not all couples felt that way.

Anna began nervously tapping her fingernail against the top of the desk. "About six months before John died, he started acting weird."

"Explain weird?"

Her eyes lingered on the keyboard, seeing beyond the assortment of letters and symbols. "He started barricading himself in his office, late-night calls became a constant, clandestine meetings took over his schedule, unmarked vehicles frequented our driveway... his existence morphed into something secretive, and his personality changed."

"In what way?"

"He was never what one might describe as a man of fervor. You know?"

Dwight raised his brows, silently stating that he didn't.

"No." She let out a little laugh that dissipated quickly. "I don't suppose a man like you would." Her eyes locked with his and in that moment, a connection was made. It was as if their minds had synced, and they were sharing the same erotic fantasy. The two of them locked in a scene of passionate love.

The thought sent electric currents coursing through Dwight's body. Where the hell had that come from? Flushed and hard, he shifted in his chair. "I get it. Go on."

Frazzled, Anna quickly regained her train of thought. "But," she continued, her voice tinged with sadness, "with these changes came an end to any physical affection towards me."

Dwight was beginning to get a clearer picture of John Tillman and he didn't like it.

Her fingers twisting and untwisting in her lap as she let out a long sigh. "It felt as though I repelled him- like he couldn't stand to even be near me. Things became so strained between us that I'd moved out and was about to call off the engagement."

It was one thing to be dedicated and fully invested in a job, but it was another to keep a woman who clearly had feelings for you holding onto false hope and rejecting her in the process.

Dwight suddenly felt like a real bastard for not putting more into that kiss she'd surprised him with. "I see."

It was clear that Anna blamed herself for John's reactions. But Dwight needed to make her understand that it wasn't her fault. No man in their right mind would be repulsed by a woman as sexy, smart and beautiful as her. But he couldn't just blurt those words out. "Maybe it was stress," he suggested.

She started vehemently shaking her head. "No."

"Was he working a difficult case?"

"No," she said again. "He hadn't worked on a case

in over a year and that's where things go from weird to dangerous."

Dwight's ears perked at the mention of danger. Anna double clicked on the camera file folder. A multitude of images fluttered across the screen. She scrolled through them until she found what she was looking for. Then, she double clicked the image to enlarge it.

A man with the scowl stood next to the suited man who Dwight assumed was Tillman. His looks were intense, with dark hair slicked back into a tight ponytail that reached his shoulders. A scruffy beard framed his stone-like jawline, radiating a dangerous vibe.

Clad in a suede jacket that molded to his toned frame, he emitted an air of peril. His stance was taut, his posture demanding attention as he looked to be scanning the area.

But it was his expression that caught Dwight's attention —a lethal scowl etched onto his face, as if daring anyone to challenge him. His eyes, dark and intense, seemed to bore into Dwight's soul with an unsettling intensity.

The man's scowl hinted at a volatile and dangerous nature simmering beneath the surface.

Anna's trembling finger singled him out, her face a mixture of terror and trepidation. "This is Malachi Wolfe. John hired him as a bodyguard."

"Why did Tillman need a bodyguard?"

She shrugged. "Beats me, but that's when all the weirdness started."

Dwight mentally assessed what she'd told him. Late-night phone calls. Unknown vehicles. Reclusiveness and Malachi Wolfe, the bodyguard. "What else do you know about Wolfe?

"Nothing except he's the man who shot John."

Dwight scooted to the edge of his seat. "Are you sure?"

She rubbed her arms, swallowing hard before she answered. "I'm positive. I saw it with my own eyes."

Dwight sprang from his seat, already reaching for his phone to dial Nolan and tell him that Anna had just gone from suspect to witness. "We'll turn this over to the sheriff."

But her sudden rise caught him off guard. He felt her grip on his hand. "There's more."

Chapter Twelve

Anna's hand on Dwight's felt like a fragile bird settling on a branch, delicate and light. The softness of her skin against his calloused palm sent an electrical spark through his body, awakening a long-forgotten sensation within him. Her hand felt small in his, but it held a comforting weight that anchored him in the present moment.

She exerted gentle pressure on her grip, guiding him back to the desk, but she didn't let go of his hand. Clicking on a different folder, she drew up a video shot from what looked like the bushes and at a distance.

"What's this?" he asked.

She paused the video. "When John started giving me the cold shoulder, I assumed there was another woman."

"Was there?" Dwight asked.

She didn't answer. Instead, she clicked the play button. "A week before he was killed, I followed him to this abandoned warehouse, thinking I'd catch him in the act."

The lens focused on the man outside the warehouse. It was unmistakably Tillman. Hands in his pockets, he scanned the area nervously. Moments later, a white van pulled up beside his black Mercedes, its rear facing the warehouse doors.

Malachi emerged from the driver's side and opened the back of the van.

Heart pounding, Dwight watched as a blindfolded young woman stumbled out, wrists bound, and face contorted with fear. "Holy shit," he whispered.

Three more women followed. All were about the same age and all blindfolded and bound at the wrists.

"Jesus, Anna," Dwight said when the video ended.

"I know what it looks like," she was quick to say.

Scrubbing a hand over his face. A multitude of emotions slammed him. Anger and disgust being at the forefront. "What it looks like is human trafficking."

"John was a good man," she defended. "He wouldn't have been involved in something so horrible."

Anna's beautiful features were pulled tight in disbelief and her fight to defend her ex-fiancé. The proof was right in front of her, but she couldn't see it. Maybe it was because she couldn't acknowledge that someone she'd been in love with had been a willing participant in something so heinous. Or maybe Tillman was innocent. Maybe Wolfe had been blackmailing him with secrets, or worse. Maybe Tillman's involvement was to protect Anna.

Dwight's focus went back to the laptop and the video. Everything about the man, his posture, body language and expression said otherwise.

John Tillman had been an evil man and a willing player in trafficking young women. Dwight was willing to bet the ranch on it.

He stood and began to pace the space in front of the desk. But all that was of little consequence now. Tillman was dead. Wolfe wasn't, which led Dwight to a different train of thought. The tracks in the snow. "Malachi knows you have the video, doesn't he?" he asked.

A look of complete terror washed over Anna's face. "Yes," she murmured before wrapping her arms around her midriff as the tears came. "When I saw John go down, I grabbed the memory card and ran to Hogue's house."

"Hey," he murmured softly, reaching out to envelop her in his arms. With tender care, he drew her close, cradling her head against his chest in a protective hold. "It's okay. No one's going to get to you here. Understand?"

His heart beat with a fierce protectiveness, his arms tightening around Anna's shaking body. The scent of her hair, wild and evocative as the meadows after a summer storm, filled his senses and grounded him in the moment. As she nestled closer, the soft curves of her body yielding to the solid strength of his, the fine tremors that racked her frame began to subside.

Dwight knew how to handle a woman's tears, to calm her fears and create an unbreakable bond of intimacy and trust. He had mastered this with Tamara, but now he found himself in unfamiliar territory with another woman in his arms. Yet he navigated it with an instinctual certainty that he was where he needed to be. Each sob that shuddered from her was met with a gentle stroke of his hand along her back, a silent reassurance that whispered through touch what words might fail to convey.

The fears that tormented Anna, the looming shadow of Malachi potentially finding her at the ranch, were like an ominous storm she couldn't outrun. But as her grip on his shirt slackened, her breathing slowly evening out, Dwight realized that trust was not just given; it was earned during times like these.

Dwight suddenly noticed how perfectly their bodies fit together. The softness of her curves pressed against the solid wall of his chest was arousing. He brushed a stray lock of hair from her face, marveling at how beautiful she was.

That fuzzy feeling was back in his brain. The one that made him woozy and lightheaded. Before, he'd tried to explain it away, but now, in this moment, there was no denying what he was feeling was love.

He was falling in love with Anna.

"I'm sorry," she said. "Your family is in danger because of me."

"Shhh," he whispered, gently lifting her face. Using his thumbs, he wiped away the tears. "You have nothing to be sorry about. You've done nothing wrong, Anna. Nothing."

She looked at him, her feelings mirroring his, her eyes darkening with passion that seared into his very being. Every muscle in his body tightened, desire pulsing through him. His dick hardened, and an overwhelming need to taste her lips consumed him.

He'd been imprisoned by his own guilt for far too long, aching for the tender touch of a woman. Stuck in a limbo of mourning, he intimately knew the misery of longing for love while being consumed by grief.

And likewise, Anna was desperate for a real connection, something Dwight suspected she hadn't felt in a while. Tillman's frigid personality had left her empty and longing, her needs ignored under his cold exterior. She yearned for the warmth of human touch, but it had been denied to her for far too long.

They were drawn together by a mutual need for companionship. The longing for physical touch and affection was palpable between them, an ache so intense that it seemed to reverberate through the room.

As Dwight's rationality crumbled under the weight of his burning need for Anna, she could only meet his gaze with a fire that rivaled his own. In that moment, nothing else mattered but the primal pull between them, driving them towards each other like magnets.

They were at a crossroads.

He could kiss her, really kiss her, the way he'd wanted to for days. Or he could drop his arms, walk away and stay that broken man, tangled in his own remorse and grief, never experiencing the ecstasy of sheathing himself inside her sweet body, or the love she had to offer him.

He chose Anna.

His lips met hers with an intensity that seemed to set the world ablaze, igniting a flame that could only be quenched by making her his.

ANNA'S SENSES ignited as Dwight's lips crushed against hers, the fervent pressure unwavering, insistent. His mouth, a molten promise, tasted like coffee with a hint of whiskey. Every inch of her tingled with an electricity she only felt in the tempestuous presence of a summer thunderstorm—or when Dwight was near.

This was the kiss she had been longing for, the kiss that unleashed Dwight's wild side. His head tilted with a hint of dominance, his tongue boldly tracing the outline of her lips, causing her to gasp in anticipation. Their tongues danced in a sensual and thrilling rhythm, igniting a fire within her that only he could tame.

Anna's arms twined around his neck, her body molding itself against his as she met his lips with an eager intensity that had been simmering since the moment she'd woke up and discovered him sleeping in the recliner.

The stubble on his jaw grazed her skin, a delightful friction that sent shivers over her. The rugged texture contrasted with the softness of his lips, a reminder of the man himself—strong and unyielding, yet capable of such gentleness. His scent enveloped her, a blend of leather, soap and the faintest touch of hay, and underneath it all, the unique essence that was undeniably Dwight.

His hands, confident and strong, slipped under her sweater. The rough pads of his fingers burned trails over her skin, tracing the arch of her back, pulling her closer until there was no space left for doubt or hesitation.

Was this happening? Was this going to be more than a kiss? She wanted it to. She wanted more of him, more of this dizzy recklessness only he could make her feel. It was all happening so quickly. She couldn't resist the pull towards him, drawn to the rough edges of his body pressing against hers. His touch was scorching, awakening desires that had long been suppressed within her, flames that only Dwight could stoke.

"This feels wrong." His words were a growl against her ear, rough and fragmented as if he was fighting an inner battle. "But at the same time, so damn right."

She could feel his pain, his desperation to hold on to a loyalty that was killing him. He needed her reassurance, her validation that this was worth it, that he wouldn't regret the night if the kiss went further. But she couldn't give him that. "I can't tell you if it's right or wrong, Dwight," she replied with equal fervor, giving into the desire coursing through their veins. "All I know is I want you."

A guttural sound escaped his lips as her fingers traced over the skin under his shirt, igniting a fire within him. "I'm tired of hurting," he murmured against her neck. "I'm tired of being alone."

Anna grabbed hold of his Stetson, slung it onto the worktable and began unbuttoning his shirt. "So am I."

And that was all the confirmation Dwight needed. He groaned and shifted, allowing her full access to do whatever she wanted. Right now, she wanted him naked.

With a flick of her fingers, she undid the last button on Dwight's shirt, revealing his sculpted torso that made her weak in the knees. Her hands roamed over his taut muscles, and she savored the sound of pleasure that escaped his lips.

He gently pulled up the hem of her sweater, exposing her supple skin. She willingly raised her arms, allowing him to remove it completely. His eyes transformed into a deep, dark blue, swirling with passion and desire as they roamed over her lace-covered breasts. A low growl escaped his lips as he reached for the clasp of her bra, desperate to set her free.

Slowly, he unhooked it, appreciating every moment of exposing her body. "You are breathtaking," he whispered huskily, before sliding the straps off her shoulders with deliberate slowness. "I've wanted to do this since I first brought you home."

Home. The word stirred more than physical desire in Anna. It made her feel like she belonged, like she was a part of his family, his life — heart and soul.

Dwight's lips traced a delicate pattern of kisses down her neck and along her collarbone. Cupping her breast in his large hand, he used the tip of his tongue to outline her areola. It was a sensual awakening that left Anna gasping for breath. "I've never..." her words were lost to pleasure.

"There's so much more I want to do to you." His

teeth nipped gently at her nipple, causing her to cry out in shock and ecstasy. His lips roamed over her skin, trailing fire wherever they touched, while her fingers tangled in his hair, pulling him ever closer. "It's going to be a long, long night, sweetheart," he said, reaching for the snap on her jeans.

She had no concept of time, day or night. There was only her cowboy, her rescuer, her protector. The man who held her heart.

Dwight popped the snap loose, found the tab of her zipper and drew it down. His fingers skillfully slipped beneath the denim waistband, guiding it along with her underwear over the curves of her hips.

He took a step back, his gaze sweeping over her naked body with longing and appreciation. "You're beautiful, Anna."

She'd never felt so loved, so empowered, or so content. "Thank you." Holding his face in her hands, she kissed him.

He tenderly, but firmly, kneaded her bottom, bringing her up and into the rough abrasion of his denim-covered cock. She arched into him, meeting his slow thrusts with a sensual rhythm that made her wet.

"You're overdressed, Mr. Murtaugh," she said, her fingers fumbling to undo his silver belt buckle.

Dwight agreed with a grunt and began kicking off his boots. Once the buckle and belt were undone, his zipper went down and off came his jeans.

It was her turn to admire, and she did. His thighs, strong and commanding, were formed from days spent in the saddle and laborious work on the ranch, powerful and sinewy, full of a strength that hinted at a latent gentleness capable of tender caresses or earth-shaking intensity.

Moving down, she marveled at his calves; they were

like something out of an ancient myth—pure masculine artistry. The bulging muscles spoke of power and agility, shaped not in an artist's studio but through years of mastering the wild terrain that had been both his playground and proving ground.

Anna's eyes teasingly lingered, soaking in every inch of the man before her, her pulse bounding in time with the appreciation that thrummed through her veins.

The dark trail of hair covering his chest seemed to beckon her fingers to explore, to chart a course over the taut, sun-kissed skin of his stomach that rippled with each breath he took.

Her regard continued its descent, drawn unavoidably to the pronounced V of his hips that pointed like arrows to the hard bulge of his erection, a jaw-dropping display of virile strength that held promises of earth-shattering pleasure.

From the untamed locks atop his dark head that begged for her fingers to entwine with them, down to the soles of his naked feet, he was the embodiment of raw masculinity.

And he was all hers.

Dwight scooped Anna up in his arms and carried her to the cot in the back. He lowered her onto the cot with a tenderness that contrasted sharply with the intensity burning in his eyes. The simple mattress accepted her weight with a soft sigh, the thick cotton cover yielding beneath her as if it were made of clouds.

He gently parted her legs, and she let out a little gasp when he positioned himself between her thighs. The head of his arousal, hot and pulsing, pressed firmly against the delicate folds of her opening.

And then he was kissing her again. Urgently, like her lips held his last chance for air. With his breath coming in broken waves and his body shaking, fighting for control, he lifted his head and looked at her.

Suddenly, an unexpected sensation came over her. Like a faint scratching at the back of her brain, fear began to claw its way through her desire addled thoughts, ripping to shreds her reasons for thinking she could wipe away all his pain and grief.

She wanted Dwight. She wanted him to make love to her, to feel him inside her, to hold her in his arms and say the words she so desperately wanted to hear.

I love you.

But there were no guarantees, no certainties that after he made love to her, he wouldn't regret it. And that was terrifying. She might lose him forever.

Anna knew she could say the word, and this would end as quickly as it had started, with Dwight retreating and them never knowing what could have been.

But she wasn't going to do that. She'd take a chance and roll that dice. Because sometimes all a woman had was luck.

Her hands tightened on his hips, her body arching towards him eagerly as he thrust himself inside of her, filling her completely.

With his eyes locked on hers and his jaw clenched tight, he withdrew slightly and plunged into her again. She let out a cry of pleasure and locked her legs around his hips.

It was exquisite and the most moving moment of her life and she didn't want it to end. But the slow-moving rhythm soon escalated to a faster beat, intensifying a blooming pleasure low in her belly that threatened to burst and consume her.

When the orgasm took hold, it was like touching the sun. She gasped, her head rolled back, and she cried out with pleasure. As her fingernails bit into the muscles of his back, Dwight closed his eyes and made the deepest, wildest guttural growl she'd ever heard.

He thrust into her one last time, his body shaking with the release and then lowered his head. Breathing heavily, he pressed a kiss to her lips. "Are you okay?"

Anna was more than okay. She was completely and utterly satisfied for the first time in her life. "I've waited my whole life to be loved like that."

A cold veneer passed across his face before he dropped his eyes and moved from her.

She instantly regretted the wording of that sentence, but it was true. And there was nothing she could do about it now except face the repercussions.

But she regretted nothing about what they'd shared —the love they'd made. And she wouldn't pretend she did.

He took a blanket from the bottom of the cot and settled in beside her then pulled her close, pressing her soft curves against his hard body as he lay back on the pillow. Resting one hand under his head, he sighed heavily and closed his eyes.

This had been their moment together, their time in the sun: a place where passion and pleasure created a cocoon of love and possibilities. And even if it lasted only until dawn, she would cherish every fleeting moment in his arms.

Chapter Thirteen

"THAT BASTARD IS BACK!" THE SHOUT JOSTLED Anna from sleep. For a moment, she thought she might be dreaming, but then she heard another one.

She sat up. "Dwight," she said, shaking him awake.

He opened his eyes and frowned, focusing on her face.

"Something's going on outside," she whispered.

He sat up, blinking and rubbing his eyes until he could focus on finding his clothes.

"Hey boss!" Three hard knocks followed Sonny's yell.

"What is it?" he answered back.

"You better get out here," was all Sonny said.

They dressed quickly. Neither saying a word about what had happened. That conversation would have to wait. Whatever was going on outside took precedence.

Dwight grabbed his hat, slid his jacket on, and hurried to the door. Anna followed, sliding her arms into the warmth of her borrowed garment as he opened the door with a harsh curse. "Goddamn it, Sonny. This better be important."

Sonny brought his rifle down from his shoulder and chambered a round. "That cougar is back."

Dwight took hold of Anna's hand and pulled her out the door while keeping her shielded behind him.

She couldn't make sense of it. She knew cougars were dangerous predators and could pose a substantial threat to livestock. But all this fuss for a cougar? It hardly seemed logical.

Unless...

That "cougar" they spoke of was clearly code for something far more sinister. Outside, the tranquility mirrored that of their earlier trek to the workshop, but now frantic hands dashed towards the opposite end of the barn.

"It looks like blood." Sonny's words struck fear into Anna. As she and Dwight trailed after him, the tension was so thick it was suffocating. The men had congregated up ahead, their hushed whispers and darting glances creating a palpable sense of intrigue. Her heart was pounding in her chest as he shone his flashlight on the wall, revealing the words written in blood letters. "I'm coming for you."

A scream escaped Anna's lips, and she stumbled backwards, fear gripping her like a vise. This couldn't be happening. "Oh, God!"

"It's paint, Anna," Dwight said, taking her firmly by the shoulders. "Calm down."

Calm. He expected her to be calm when Malachi had all but written her death sentence in big, blood-read letters? She smacked his hands away as panic overtook her. "Don't you see? It's him! He's found me!"

"He's just trying to scare you," Dwight told her, matching her steps as she backtracked towards the ranch truck parked nearby.

Someone let out a loud whistle. The sound carried from a distance was followed by an, "Over here!"

"What now?" Dwight asked, turning to see two of

his ranch hands in a nearby pasture standing with their rifles aimed at a man lying face-down in the snow.

"We got him!" Anna heard Carl yell and hold up a sidearm like it was a trophy.

"Malachi?" she asked, nearly stiff with fear. "They've got Malachi?"

Dwight nonchalantly brushed his jacket back to reveal the gun holstered at his side. "You stay put," he commanded sternly, handing her off to Sonny. "And you, don't let her out of your sight."

"I won't."

The ramrod, though sufficiently armed and physically capable of holding his own in a gunfight, did little to ease Anna's mind.

Malachi was strong, devious and ruthless and would stop at nothing to get his hands on that memory card. She wouldn't feel safe until he was either dead or behind bars.

The moon hung heavy and low, a luminous spectator in the midnight sky, casting an eerie glow over the scene unfolding beneath it.

There were well over a dozen armed cowboys ready to shoot first and ask questions later, but Anna wasn't letting her guard down. If the man Dwight's ranch hands had subdued was Malachi, she knew he wouldn't go down without a fight.

"Get him up," Dwight said, his voice devoid of trepidation, but Anna knew better. The caution in his steps belied his tone, his eyes never wavering from Malachi's subdued form. "I want to see his face."

Carl, too cocky for his own good, latched hold of the man's collar. "You heard the boss. Get up!"

Malachi was a shadow that dwelt in unexpected corners, a cunningly cloaked danger wrapped in a facade of defeat. As Anna's eyes focused in on the man, the silvery moonlight caught on the slick edge of a hunting knife in Malachi's hand, turning the blade into a sinister streak of quicksilver.

"No!" The word tore from her throat as if it could somehow alter fate. Another scream forced itself from her as the moonlight danced off the blade just before it buried itself into Carl's thigh.

Carl let out a shriek of agony, dropped his rifle and clutched his thigh before falling to the ground. Displaying deftness and exactitude, Malachi swiftly retracted the blade, whirled around in a smooth motion, and landed the weapon into the flank of another unsuspecting ranch hand.

With both men down and Dwight running towards them, Malachi pointed the blade, dripping dark with blood at Anna.

It was as if her worst nightmare had suddenly come to life and the devil himself was staring her down.

"You're next, bitch!" Malachi yelled as his sinister figure disappeared into the darkness of the trees. The dense forest swallowed him whole, its shadows cloaking his escape.

The ranch was no longer safe for any of them. Malachi's threat had just become up close and personal. Dwight, Lael and Liam were in danger because of her. She couldn't stay. She had to run. Malachi would follow her, and they'd be safe.

Anna could hear shots being fired and men yelling, but her mind was on getting away from Sonny and to the truck parked nearby.

She stepped back, spun around and made a mad dash towards the truck, her heart thudding against her ribcage. What happened next was like a dream, a nightmare that she couldn't wake from. A force so hard she could only describe it as the hand of God slammed into her. It catapulted her back and into the air. After what seemed like an eternity suspended in inertia, she landed hard against the cold earth.

And then there was only darkness. Then somewhere in the deep recess of her mind, she heard her name. It was a voice full of fear and desperation.

"Anna!" It was Dwight. "God, no," he whispered softly against her ear as he pleaded. "Please don't do this to me again."

Do what? Why couldn't she move? Or speak? Or breathe?

As the question escaped his lips, her chest convulsed, causing her to greedily inhale a breath. She hacked and wheezed, desperate for more air.

"That a girl," she heard Lael say.

"The sheriff is on his way," said a male voice from somewhere in the distance.

"And an ambulance!" Dwight yelled. "Tell them to hurry!"

A dull pain hit Anna in the ribs. She groaned and tried opening her eyes, but her lids felt like they were glued shut.

"Oh, thank God." Dwight's voice was raspy against her lips as he cradled her head in his hands. "I thought I'd lost you, sweetheart."

Lost her? What did he mean? Who was hurt? Who needed the ambulance? Her mind searched for answers and in the darkness, she saw a boy. A child she loved. "L-Liam?"

"He's fine," Dwight answered, a flood of relief in his voice. As the soft bristles of his beard brushed against her cheek, she felt something wet against her face.

Tears.

Why was Dwight crying? With that question, the

darkness overtook her again, and she felt nothing but peace.

THE STERILE SCENT of the hospital mingled with the sharp tang of antiseptic solutions as Anna's gurney was pushed through the bustling corridors. Her senses, dulled by the shockwave from the truck explosion, began to sharpen under the fluorescent glare of the overhead lights. Each bulb seemed to buzz with an intensity that matched the erratic thrumming of her heart.

She blinked against the harsh light, trying to focus on the faces that swooped into view, then disappeared just as quickly. Their features blurred and faded to black as she went in and out of consciousness.

As she was transferred onto an E.R. bed, the coolness of the crisp, white sheets contrasted sharply with her skin, still tingling from the blast's heat. Doctors and nurses crowded around her, their voices a mix of urgency and commands. A nurse with gentle eyes and steady hands inserted an IV line into Anna's arm; the slight pinch was a grounding point in the madness that seemed to be overtaking her.

"Stay with us, Anna," one doctor said, his voice low and resonant—an anchor in the middle of the flurry of medical jargon being exchanged over her prone form. When he stepped away, she could see that he wore cowboy boots under his scrubs. It was an unexpected sight that oddly comforted her, reminding her of home.

Home. The word evoked a wave of emotions and memories. The comforting scent of burning logs, the cozy warmth emanating from the crackling fireplace. The rich, mouthwatering flavors of Lael's home-style cooking. The sweet sound of Liam's infectious laughter echoing through the halls of the ranch house. Dwight's strong arms, holding her as he made tender love to her.

Oh, how she wanted to go home.

Her clothing was carefully cut away, replaced by a hospital gown that felt too light and insubstantial against her bruised body. The scent of her own scorched fabric mixed with the astringency in the air, making her stomach churn. Every touch from the medical staff was professional, but under each clinical brush of their fingers, a latent awareness of her vulnerability pulsed.

Anna's thoughts drifted in and out, punctuated by the needle-sharp pain that lanced through her every time she drew a breath. It felt as if her ribs were protesting each expansion of her lungs, yet beneath the physical distress, another sensation always surfaced—a warmth not born of injury but of memory.

Each time, she felt like she was slipping away, she thought of Dwight's strong arms, remembered how they'd enveloped her in moments of passion and comfort alike.

Her mind wandered back to the last time they'd been together minutes before the accident in his workshop. His lovemaking had been hungry yet tender, an intoxicating mix that had left her feeling both cherished and desired. The softness of his lips, the roughness of his strong hands loving her so completely.

But with those treasured memories came the haunting image of regret as it registered across his handsome face. She couldn't bear that heartache, not now when her body and soul were so weak. She chose, instead, to focus on the love they'd shared.

In a haze between consciousness and sleep, Anna clung to those memories. Those were as clear and visceral as if Dwight were right there beside her, his presence a reassuring weight against the darkness that surrounded her. She could almost hear his voice—a low, comforting drawl that she'd come to associate with safety and love. It was this blend of dreams and reality that kept her tethered to the present as pain medication dripped steadily into her veins.

A nurse adjusted something on a monitor, and the beeping seemed to sync with Anna's heartbeat, lulling her into a half-dream state where she could feel Dwight's breath against her neck, whispering promises that mingled with his tears.

Time lost meaning as she floated on the edge of consciousness. When she finally stirred back to full awareness, she found herself alone in a private room with moonlight spilling through a slit in the blind.

The air in the room shifted and Anna realized she wasn't alone. As her gaze lingered on the forlorn figure in the corner, she felt a pull of sympathy overriding her own pain. With great effort, she pushed herself up into a sitting position, the blanket pooled at her waist. The sight of Dwight – her strong, steadfast cowboy – looking so vulnerable hurt worse than her ribs.

"Dwight?" Her voice was a raspy whisper.

He looked up sharply. Shadows played across his face, accentuating the lines of worry and exhaustion that had settled there. He rose to his feet with a smoothness that contrasted his earlier posture of defeat and moved toward her. "I'm here," he said, taking her hand.

"Malachi—"

"Don't talk," he said, hushing her with a tender kiss on the lips. "You're okay. That's all that matters. Rest now. I'll be here when you wake up."

Would he? Fear and uncertainty about what lay ahead for them overtook her as she closed her eyes. Her body felt leaden and broken, but it was her heart that ached the most.

Chapter Fourteen

"How is she?" Nolan asked, his eyes a mixture of concern and regret as he motioned for Dwight to take a seat across from the desk.

Dwight sat down, pushed the brim of his Stetson up, and pressed his palms against his eyes, feeling them burn from worry and exhaustion. "A bump on the head and a few bruised ribs."

"She was lucky," Nolan said.

Dwight's mind played the scene over, the roar of the explosion that had sent a shockwave through the ranch, the way his heart had plummeted to his boots at the sight of Anna's silhouette outlined against the flames of the explosion, her body flung backward with brutal force. "I should have seen this coming."

Nolan leaned back, his chair creaking under the weight of the unsaid. No one, including the sheriff, had taken the threat against Anna seriously. "What happened blindsided all of us."

Dwight wasn't going to make excuses. One of his ranch hands was in critical condition and the other would have to undergo months of physical therapy just to walk again. He didn't want to think about what

Malachi would have done to Anna if they hadn't stopped him. "She could have died, Nolan."

"But she didn't," he reminded him.

The scene had been pure chaos when Nolan and a swarm of deputies and first responders descended upon the ranch minutes after the truck explosion. As EMTs frantically worked to stabilize Anna for transport, Dwight hastily briefed Nolan on the situation and handed over the crucial memory card.

With the arrival of FBI agents, it became clear that Copper Creek and Harmony were just small pieces in a much larger puzzle of human trafficking. Discovered to be someone in charge within the organization, John Tillman's involvement as well as other Harmony officials who'd taken bribes to look the other way were being investigated.

Thanks to Anna's footage and bravery, authorities had located the warehouse and rescued the women, and they now had a name and face to go with Tillman's killer: Malachi Wolfe was a notorious criminal with a rap sheet a mile long. Nolan and his team had set up road-blocks, and a statewide manhunt was underway for Malachi's capture. But if he managed to slip through their fingers, Dwight was determined to make sure justice would still be served.

His gut was telling him Malachi hadn't left Copper Creek, and that Anna was still very much in danger. This was the first time he'd left her side since she'd been rushed to the hospital two days ago. He was hesitant about leaving her, even with a deputy guarding her door, but Nolan had insisted this meeting couldn't wait.

Dwight was anxious to get Anna home. Back to the Sweet Surrender where, this time, he would protect her. "I should have listened to her when she told me Malachi was dangerous. Instead, I trusted my own ignorance about the situation."

"You're not the only one who feels like they dropped the ball on this one," Nolan said, rolling his jaw from side to side. "But all we can do now is move forward."

Dwight, his concern more about his relationship with Anna than the ongoing investigation, wasn't sure how to do that. Guilt seemed to come at him from all sides, scrambling his thinking and weighing heavily on his heart. A man was supposed to be there for the woman he loved. It was his duty, his honor, to keep her safe and protect her at all costs.

Dwight would have gladly traded his life for Tamara's. Instead, he'd been too goddamn busy to answer the phone when she'd called him for a ride that night.

He'd begged God for another chance to make things right, to let it all be a horrific dream that he could wake from. But after months of pleading, he'd finally faced the truth, the reality that living without Tamara, was his penance.

But then, beautiful, sweet Anna had come into his life. His heart had been on the verge of healing, and he'd been on the cusp of self-forgiveness. He realized that now. Everything was crystal clear to Dwight. He could see how much Anna had changed him. They'd made love, sweet, sweet love. His heart had righted itself and he had a chance for happiness.

That was, until the explosion. Not once, but twice, he'd failed to be there when the woman he was in love with needed him. What kind of man was he, if he couldn't protect the people he loved?

"How's Lael holding up?" Nolan's voice penetrated Dwight's train of thought.

"You know Lael," he said, his focus shifting to the

mass of black suits outside Nolan's office. "She's ready to round up a posse and go after Malachi."

Nolan chuckled. "Well, at least you don't have to worry about her and Liam during all of this."

"Yeah," Dwight agreed, knowing they'd be safe at Brian and Stacey's house until Malachi was in custody. "I need to get back to the hospital. They're releasing Anna at noon, so can we get on with this? Why'd you call me in here?"

Nolan slid on his reading glasses and opened the file lying in front of him. "We have statements from everyone there that night, but I wanted to make sure you hadn't thought of anything else."

"I haven't," Dwight said.

Using his finger as a guideline, Nolan read part of Dwight's statement aloud. "You said when your men caught up with Malachi in the north pasture, you left Anna with Sonny."

"That's right," he affirmed. "I wanted to make sure it was Malachi, and I didn't want her near him when I did."

"Because you'd just watched the video and knew you could identify him?"

"Yes."

Nolan removed his bifocals. "So, Anna wasn't anywhere near Malachi, or was the gun Carl took from him?"

"No," Dwight said, frowning. "She was with Sonny the whole time. Why?"

Nolan sighed and rubbed his eyes. "The ballistics report came back. The bullet is a match."

Nolan liked taking the scenic route on his way to making a point. But Dwight wasn't in the mood to entertain his ambling rambles. "That should make your job easier."

"You'd think so, wouldn't you?" Nolan said sarcastically. "But no."

"Why not?"

"You were the only one close enough to identify him and even then, it was dark."

"It was him," Dwight stated firmly.

"Sorry, but I needed indisputable proof that Malachi Wolfe came into my county, vandalized property and nearly killed three of my constituent's."

Dwight wondered what Nolan's feathers had ruffled. The man was dry and unbendable, but he never lost his cool. "Okay, but you still haven't answered my question." He stood up, ready to walk out the door if he didn't get a straight answer. "What am I here?"

Nolan strode back around his desk to pick up the file, opened it, took out a piece of paper, and handed it to Dwight. "Because when we dusted Malachi's gun, we not only found his prints, but Anna's too."

Dwight stared down at the report, dumbfounded by the damming piece of evidence in his hands. "What?"

"A one on the grip and on the trigger."

"Are you sure?" Dwight asked, believe this to be all a mistake.

"Her prints were put into the system in Harmony. They're a match. She fired that gun, Dwight."

"No."

"The evidence says otherwise." Nolan tossed the file into a drawer and slammed it shut. "I'm sorry, but this puts us right back where we started."

"With Anna being a suspect in both deaths." Dwight raked off his hat and ran his fingers through his hair, feeling defeated on so many levels. But at the same time, confused. "I don't get it. Why hasn't the FBI marched into the hospital and handcuffed her to the bed yet?"

Nolan, looking uncharacteristically uncomfortable in his element, shifted in his seat. "Because they don't know about the prints—yet."

Holy shit. Nolan Blackfeather was keeping a key piece of evidence from the FBI? What dimension had they shifted into?

"I don't understand," Dwight said. "You're a by-the-book man."

"I'm not making the same mistake twice," he said.

Dwight smiled as the answer dawned on him. "You don't think she did it, do you?"

"It doesn't matter what I think," Nolan shot back. "But the way I see it, after all Anna has done to expose what's going on in Harmony, she deserves the benefit of the doubt."

"You big softy," Dwight mocked, relieved Anna had been granted a temporary reprieve.

Nolan ignored the remark, reached into the top drawer of his desk, and pulled out a card. He handed it to Dwight. "Hogue's body has been released for burial. I can keep a lid on this until the funeral, but after that..."

"I get it." Dwight opened the door as he pocketed the business card of the only funeral home in their small town. "Thanks, Nolan."

"For what it's worth, I do think she's innocent."

"Me too," Dwight said on his way out of the office. "Now, he just had to prove it."

Chapter Fifteen

THE SNOW THAT HAD FALLEN OVERNIGHT wasn't much, but the Sweet Surrender still lay blanketed in a thick quilt of virgin snow when Anna and Dwight returned to the ranch after picking up her prescription from the pharmacy.

Anna stood in front of the kitchen window, watching the white expanse unbroken except for the solitary trail left by Dwight's pickup as he drove down the gravel road behind the house that led to the barn.

Her gaze shifted to the charred remains of the other truck, now little more than a twisted skeleton of metal and ash. The pungent smell of burnt rubber and oil lingered in the air, an acrid reminder of the explosion that had consumed the vehicle whole and nearly taken her life. The ground around where the truck had been lay scorched, blades of brown grass transformed into blackened stubs that snapped underfoot.

It was hard not to be sad after everything that had happened over the course of the last month. She'd endured enough violence, death and criminal investigations to last a lifetime. But now she was experiencing another kind of loss, one she feared her broken heart would never recover from.

Anna rubbed her arms. The winter air clung to everything with an icy grasp, biting at any exposed skin and creeping under doors to nip at the warmth within. She could feel the chill seeping into her bones, a coldness that mirrored the distance growing between her and Dwight.

He hadn't said more than a couple of sentences on the way home, and those had been about Hogue's funeral. After making sure she was safely inside and comfortable with a warm fire burning, Dwight had gone outside to help with the evening ranch chores. She knew it was an excuse, but there was little she could do about his detached demeanor now.

Maybe in a few days, after her body was stronger, she'd confront him about what had happened between them.

Turning away as his truck disappeared behind the barn, Anna walked into the living room. The spacious room was awash in the orange glow of the fading sun as it streamed through the large windows, casting long shadows across the hardwood floors. In better times, the room would be alive with Lael's laughter and Liam's playful shrieks, but now their absence was like an open wound, raw and pulsing with longing. The silence magnified every creak of the settling house and every sigh Anna uttered into the emptiness around her.

She was restless and on the verge of wandering outside, something he'd explicitly told her not to do. Malachi hadn't been found and knowing he was out there somewhere both terrified and angered her.

She was innocent. He was a criminal. Yet he remained free while she was confined to the house. A dull ache settled in her chest, born from a combination of frustration and confinement. Knowing she was being petty and childish and should be counting her blessings instead of complaining, Anna started roaming the house for something to do.

Her fingers brushed against the smooth leather of the couch, trailed along the cool glass of framed photographs on the mantle, and finally came to rest on the worn wicker of a sewing basket tucked away in a corner.

A vivid recollection wafted through her psyche - Dwight's shirt was missing a button. She could still hear his deep drawl as he mentioned how it had popped off and rolled under the table. It was just a missing button, but maybe a subtle sign that perhaps there was a purpose to be found within these walls after all.

Going to the door, she scooted the table out and saw the button. "Gotcha," she murmured. Holding it tightly in her hand, she hurried up the stairs and into Dwight's bedroom.

The delicate scent of lavender and vanilla lingered in the air, almost as if Tamara were just beyond sight, ready to walk back into the room she had tenderly curated. A silk robe cascaded from the closet door like a waterfall of memories, its sleeves slightly fluttering in the breeze from the slow whirl of the ceiling fan. The matching slippers, nestled together, bore the shape of their former owner's feet, imprints that whispered of chilly mornings and cozy nights.

And there it was - a silver-framed photograph of Tamara, her smile frozen in time, eyes filled with laughter and love, directed at the man whose heart she still seemingly held. It was perched on the nightstand amidst a garden of glass perfume bottles and small trinkets that sparkled like dewdrops in the fading sun darting through the curtains.

A lump formed in Anna's throat, a reminder that no matter how she tried, she would always be just a footnote in a story where the previous chapters were filled with love and never-ending loyalty. She stood among the ruins of a man's life she could never truly belong to - her purpose of sewing buttons and mending clothes now reduced to a mere afterthought in the face of such intense emotions.

Holding back tears, she frantically searched the room until her eyes landed on the laundry bin. Spotting the shirt with the missing button, she snatched it up and made a swift exit from the room, her decision to leave the ranch firmly made.

Once the shirt was mended, she pressed it tenderly against her chest for a stolen moment before taking it to the washer. She measured the laundry detergent and softener, then hit the start button.

Knowing she couldn't put off the task any longer, she walked to the living room, pulled out the business card Dwight had given her from her pocket, and took a deep breath. Her fingers trembled as they danced across the worn keys of the landline phone, the digits connecting her to the funeral home.

The conversation that followed was a delicate dance between professionalism and empathy. The funeral director's tone held a warmth that felt both alien and necessary; he walked her through options with respect and patience that she hadn't known she needed. As they discussed urns—simple, dignified options that would have suited Hogue, Anna nearly broke down.

Later, she told herself. Right now, she had to focus. When Hogue's arrangements were complete, she hung up and considered her options one last time.

The Brewster house was unlivable, and her bank account had been seized by Harmony authorities when she became a suspect in John's murder. The only money she had was the money Hogue had left her. That would get her to wherever her next assignment was and give her something to live on until she got back on her feet financially.

Anna could hear the hum of the washing machine as it made its final spin, and finally, its robotic beep signaling the end of the cycle.

With the phone clutched in her hand and her heart breaking at the thought of pulling up roots before they'd had time to grow in a place she now considered home, she walked to the laundry room, opened the lid, and took out Dwight's shirt. She held it to her nose and inhaled, the faint scent of him still clinging to clean fabric.

She didn't want to leave, but she couldn't stay at the ranch. She loved Dwight, but she couldn't compete with a dead woman. Tossing the shirt into the dryer, she set the time and pushed the start button, then punched in the numbers she knew by heart and waited. The dial tone broke and Blake's familiar voice filled her ear. "Yo, Annie," he said. "What's up?"

"I need work," she said without preamble. "You got anything for me?"

There was a brief silence on the line, then Blake replied in his smooth, understanding tone, "Let me see what I can do. Might have something in the Tetons in a week or two."

Her eyes drifted to the window where the vast expanse of the ranch stretched out beneath a perfect horizon. She imagined capturing the rawness of untamed nature — the thought alone reigniting a spark within her.

But a week or two?

"That long?"

"Sorry, it's the best I can do."

Hogue's ashes wouldn't be ready for at least a week, and this was the only job she could snag on such short notice. What choice did she have? "Okay. I'll take it."

"You sure?"

"Yes," she said more firmly now. "Yes, that's exactly what I need."

After confirming details and hanging up, she felt an unexpected surge of energy. With purposeful steps, she returned to the living room.

Everything was set. All she had to do now was tell Dwight she was leaving. That shouldn't be hard to do, considering he probably wanted her gone.

And with Malachi still on the loose, leaving was the best way to keep Dwight and the others out of harm's way. It could have been him who'd been injured in that explosion. Or worse, he could have been driving the truck.

Anna didn't want to think about that. Her stomach rumbled, calling attention to its empty state. She wasn't in the mood for eating and could barely boil water, but she had to eat if she wanted to regain her strength.

Surely, Lael had something she could heat up in the microwave. The pantry was a gold mine of convenience, stacked high with cans and boxes. Her hand paused over the family-size can of chicken noodle soup; its label promised comfort in bold, warm letters. It was a simple choice, practical even, and oh, so tasty.

Plus, it was hard to ruin a pre-made meal. She quickly set about the task and in minutes she had a steaming bowl of hearty, heart-warming, good-for-the-soul chicken soup.

But soup without company, Dwight's company in particular, wasn't as tasty as she thought it would be. The food sat in her stomach like a sludge of dirty sink water.

Her ribs hurt, and her temples were starting to ping

with a low throb. She carefully halved one of the potent painkillers the doctor had prescribed her, fully aware of her body's sensitivity to such drugs. She wanted to be awake when Dwight finally made it in.

The night had settled over the ranch like a heavy woolen blanket, suffocating and thick with unspoken words. Anna snagged a knitted Afghan from the back of the couch and eased out onto the porch, her breath misting in the frigid air as she watched the last rays of sun dip below the horizon. It left behind a sky streaked with purples and oranges, a beauty that seemed at odds with her jumbled emotions.

Stepping from the porch, she walked around the house and stopped. The lights of Dwight's workshop were on. She wanted to hurry inside, retreat into the warmth of their cocoon and repeat the love they'd made. She yearned to feel his arms wrap around her, hold her and tell her everything was going to be alright.

But she knew that wouldn't happen now.

Her eyes welled with tears as she made her way back into the house. Her hands trembled as she retrieved his shirt from the dryer, folding it with care before setting it on the table next to the bowl of soup she had prepared for Dwight.

The half-pill began to work its magic, numbing not just the physical pain but also dulling the sharp edges of her worry—at least momentarily. She wondered if she should've let it hurt a bit more, if pain was a necessary companion to the truth.

In her relaxed state, she realized there was one more truth to reveal to Dwight. Would he even care? And what was the point? The authorities had the memory card, and according to the conversation she'd overheard between him and Nolan at the hospital, Harmony's secrets were being uncovered. The most surprising being John's involvement in it all.

She didn't want to think about John or Malachi or why Hogue had died. But she did. Even in sleep, it haunted her.

Anna's consciousness teetered on the edge of a chasm, the dream weaving through her mind like smoke curling from a dying fire. The shadows in her mind stretched and twisted, her pain-medicated thoughts blurring the lines between what was real and the phantoms lurking in her fevered imagination.

The images that flickered before her were disjointed, yet vivid—their colors muted as if viewed through a sepia lens. She felt the rumble of Hogue's truck under her fingertips as she gripped the steering wheel, heard the gravel crunch beneath its tires, and saw the weary green of the Montana state line sign as it loomed before them. The rest stop emerged from her memories—a desolate island marooned in an ocean of trees, where anxiety seeped into her bones like cold rain.

Her body tensed unbidden, muscles coiling as if to spring, each breath hitching in her chest. The figure of Malachi loomed in that restless dreamscape, his sinister silhouette a familiar nightmare that stalked her sleep. But as he drew nearer, morphing through the haze of her medicated stupor, Anna's heart stuttered. It wasn't Malachi's face that emerged from the shadow.

It was the face of a dead man. A ghost rising from the ashes of Harmony.

Chapter Sixteen

Dwight inserted his key into the lock, wincing as the metallic tumblers clicked loudly when he turned the deadbolt. It was past midnight when he stepped through the front door. He reset the lock and eased out of his jacket and boots, feeling as if he were shedding some part of himself in the process.

The house was quiet, as he knew it would be with Lael and Liam at Brian's. There'd been no word from the sheriff about Malachi's whereabouts. Dwight knew there was a good chance they might never find the man if he made the Canadian boarder.

Hanging his hat on the hook, he raked a hand through his hair, removed the pistol from the holster at his side, checked the safety, and placed it on the shelf above the coat rack. Then he eased into the kitchen. He hadn't felt like eating, but the hint of something hearty and inviting tugged at his taste buds.

As he flipped on the light, his heart stopped in his chest. There, sitting on the table, was what looked like a bowl of soup. And beside it, folded with care and precision, was his favorite shirt.

He couldn't believe his eyes. His appetite vanished as he ran a hand over the fabric, feeling the smooth texture of freshly washed cotton. As he unfolded the shirt, he noticed something different — the missing button was now perfectly reattached. A wave of emotions flooded him — confusion, disbelief, and dare he say it, longing.

"Sweetheart," he whispered. It was just a shirt, a missing button and a thoughtful notion from a woman who had unexpectedly become his everything. More than that, it was a representation of how far he'd come at letting Tamara go.

He'd spent all afternoon and most of the night coming to terms with his feelings for Anna. They'd made love, and she'd all but told him she loved him, leaving him raw, vulnerable, and questioning everything he thought he knew. He couldn't run from her or the emotions she stirred up inside him - a dangerous combination that made him face the darkest corners of his heart.

When he'd seen her lifeless body lying in the snow, her face bloody from the debris blast, her clothes singed from the heat, he'd felt his heart shatter into a million pieces. Then she'd started breathing and his whole world had changed. It was as if that first life-saving breath she'd sucked in had jumpstarted his dead heart into beating again. He'd realized then just how much he loved her and desperately wanted a life with her.

He returned the shirt to its place on the table, his fingers lingering for a moment longer in a final tender touch. A week ago, the mere sight of that shoddily mended shirt would have sent him into a fit of anger. The thought of another woman in Tamara's home, handling her possessions and invading his cherished memories of her, had felt like a betrayal.

But now, that seemed like pure idiocy. Dwight had lost so much but felt like he'd also gained the world. He had a chance for a new beginning with Anna. The world was a cruel place, always ready to snatch away any glimmer of happiness. But then he met Anna. And suddenly, the possibility of a new beginning seemed real again. All he had to do was stretch out his hand and take hold of it. And he was damn well going to try.

But before he could claim this newfound happiness, there were things he had to take care of first. Tamara was Liam's mother, and Lael's daughter, after all. She would always have a place in their lives. The guilt of not answering her call that fateful night would always weigh on him. He would always carry love for her in his heart. But he couldn't move on with Anna while still holding onto Tamara's ghost. He owed it to Anna, and himself, to let go and start anew.

His heart swelled with determination as he set off to find Anna. He couldn't let her slip away, not again. There were words he needed to say, feelings he needed to express.

I love you. Don't leave. Stay with me, with us...

But the moment his sock feet hit the living room floor, he knew something wasn't right. As his eyes scan the dimly lit room, an ominous feeling hitting him in the stomach like it had seconds before the truck exploded.

There on the coffee table sat Anna's bottle of pain pills along with a glass of water and a discarded Afghan.

"Anna," he called out, but only silence answered him. Thinking she might be in the bathroom, he started down the hall when he felt something wet soak into the bottom of his sock.

His hand fumbled in the darkness, searching for the light switch. "God, no," he muttered, as his eyes adjusted to the dimness. The unmistakable shape of those same boot prints he'd seen in the snow were now wet tracks on the wooden floor. "Malachi," he growled, the rush of adrenaline slamming into his body like a runaway train.

"Anna!" Dwight bolted, tracing his steps towards the guest bedroom and finally to the shattered window, where fragments of glass littered the floor.

But how? How had he gotten past the men and into the house? Whirling on his heels, he raced back to the front door and hastily shoved his feet into his boots. Snatching up his jacket and hat, he made a quick grab for his pistol. He sprinted to his truck and grabbed a flashlight from the door.

Dwight aimed the light near the busted window in search of the boot prints. There was only one set, which meant Malachi must have carried Anna from the house. An easy task, considering she was probably too groggy to fight him off thanks to the pain meds. But the tracks didn't lead towards the wood line as Dwight had expected them to. They led towards the driveway.

His fingers trembled as he fumbled for his cell phone and frantically dialed Nolan's number, heart pounding in his chest.

It rang three times. "I was just about to call you," Nolan said, weariness in his voice. "We found Malachi."

Dwight stopped and let his hand fall to his side as relief flooded his body. "Thank God. How's Anna? Is she hurt? Tell her I'm on my way."

"Anna? Why would she be—" Nolan stopped mid-question. "What's happened, Dwight?"

It was clear that he and the sheriff weren't on the same page. "Anna is gone."

"What do you mean, she's gone?" Alarm now penetrated Nolan's tone.

"Malachi busted out a window," he said, the dots in his head slowly connecting. "He came in while she was sleeping and took her."

"Son of a bitch," Nolan swore. "Dwight, Malachi is dead."

Dead? He raised the flashlight and re-centered the beam on the tracks. "Are you sure?"

Nolan scoffed. "Pretty damn sure. A trucker found him. His body was in a dumpster out by the Mountain Peak Truck Stop. He's been shot in the head at point blank range."

"No."

"Afraid so and Dwight?"

"Yeah?" he answered, dread swarming inside him.

"The coroner says he's been dead for a couple of days."

Dwight's chest constricted, the air forced from his lungs as he absorbed the shocking news. If Malachi was dead, then who had taken Anna? He felt like someone had walked over his grave as the gravity of the situation sank in.

"Shit, Dwight," Nolan said. "You know what that means?"

"Someone else has Anna," he said, feeling every muscle in his body tense.

"The FBI raided the warehouse and everyone else involved in the case is either dead or in custody?"

The bereavement conversation he'd had with Anna flashed through his mind. *Before leaving Harmony, I thought I saw John.* "Tillman," he blurted out, racing towards his truck as fast as his legs would carry him.

"Tillman is dead."

"Anna said she thought she saw him in Harmony before she and Hogue left town."

"What?" Nolan asked and Dwight heard the muffled sound of voices. "Hold on a second."

Dwight cursed under his breath as he started the engine and peeled out onto the road. Snow was falling heavily now, covering any trace that might have led them to Anna. Their only hope lay in finding her before it was too late.

"Dwight?" Nolan's voice crackled through the phone, pulling him back from his thoughts. "Are you there?"

Dwight grunted in response.

"We just got a tip of a reckless driver," Nolan said, and Dwight could hear him slamming the door of his cruiser. "If you're right, it might be Tillman."

A glimmer of hope mingled with the fear inside Dwight's chest. Pushing the gas pedal down, he disregarded the tracks and guided the truck towards the main road. "Where was the driver reported?"

There was a brief pause before Nolan replied with a hint of hesitation, "Shadow Canyon."

Dwight's throat went dry. He hadn't set foot on that cursed road since Tamara's accident. He'd avoided it for so long, unable to face the painful memories of the bridge where she took her last breath. But now, with Anna's life on the line, he'd gladly face those demons to save her.

ANNA'S GROGGY lids fluttered open to the sight of fluffy, feather-like snowflakes hitting the windshield. The headlights cast a bright beam across the snowy road, creating a blurry white path ahead. The only sound in the otherwise silent cab was the scraping and swishing of the rubber blades against the glass.

She slowly turned her head, her eyes narrowed in suspicion as they landed on the driver. She briefly remembered heating soup and mending Dwight's shirt, but all the other memories were hazy and disjointed. Had she really been snatched by some ghost?

She must have died and gone straight to hell. Because what other explanation could there be for seeing John, her dead ex-fiancé, sitting next to her in the truck, wearing a fur-lined coat and Resistol hat? Was this some sort of twisted punishment, trapped in an eternal winter with a man who had always been cold and heartless? Or was she just losing her mind? Either way, it was enough to make her want to scream or cry. Maybe both.

"This doesn't have to end badly for you, Anna," he said, keeping his cold stare training on the road. "Just give me the memory card and I'll be on my way."

She wanted to let out a derisive chuckle at his cluelessness, but she wasn't about to waste her time enlightening him. If he had any inkling that she had already handed over the disk to the sheriff days ago, he'd probably snap and leave her lifeless body in some forgotten ravine. She wasn't going to give him that satisfaction. "I don't believe in ghosts."

Dwight must have realized she was gone by now. She clung to that thought like a lifeline. If anyone could find her and protect her from John's murderous intentions, it was him.

The truck swerved as John made a curve too fast. "I tried to keep you sheltered from the business, but—"

"Business?" she snapped back, clutching the door handle when she felt the truck slide over the yellow line. "You were buying and selling people, John! How could you think that was business?"

"Framing you for my murder wasn't my idea," he said, disregarding her question. "But Malachi thought you were getting too close. I hope you can forgive me."

"Forgive you?" she asked, incredulously. "You almost destroyed my life and Hogue is dead because of you!"

John made a tittering sound with his tongue. "You can't blame me for that. You were the one who shot Hogue."

"Bastard," she seethed and settled deeper into the seat. It occurred to her then that if John was doing his own dirty work, Malachi must be in jail or worse.

She felt a tiny bit of justice about that.

"The memory card," he insisted again. "Where is it?"

She couldn't help but shiver as the ghostly shape of a bridge came into view. This had to be Shadow Canyon. Tamara had gone over that bridge, and now Anna wondered if she would meet the same fate. Her only chance was to jump out of the truck and make a run for it. John's slow driving due to the snow gave her a small window of opportunity, but it had to be timed perfectly if she wanted to escape.

She'd distract John, then jump from the truck, and if she didn't die when she hit the pavement, she'd hide. Maybe she could dive into the water and swim to safety. An involuntary shiver hit her body. She'd been there and done that and she didn't want to do it again. But if that was her only chance, she'd take it. "For a man who was smart enough to hide his shady business dealings from authorities and the woman he was supposed to be in love with, you sure are clueless."

His eyes darted to her, then back to the road. "What are you talking about?"

"You're such a self-absorbed jackass," she hissed, her fingers tightening around the door handle. "Where have you been hiding? In a hole? I handed over the evidence to the sheriff. They know it all, John. The warehouse, the women... Your dirty little secret is finally exposed."

His jaw tightened. "You bitch."

"With Malachi gone, there's no sacrificial lamb to take the blame for my murder." She spat out the last word, bitterness seeping into every syllable.

John eased off the gas and leveled her with a smug grin. "Oh, honey, don't fret," he drawled, his hand brushing her cheek. "Offing you would be such a shame. A pretty little thing like yourself could fetch a mighty penny."

The realization hit her like a punch to the gut. That man, who she had once thought was her everything, now made her stomach churn with disgust. She couldn't believe that she had ever loved him. But then again, she had never truly known love until Dwight came into her life. He had set the bar high, and no one else could compare. If she managed to survive this ordeal, she knew she would spend the rest of her days alone, because no other man could ever hold a candle to Dwight's love.

As the thought seared through her mind like a branding iron, she whipped her head around and sank her teeth into John's finger, drawing blood. His high-pitched scream of pain was music to her ears as he released the steering wheel in shock. Revenge was sweet, and she relished in it.

Chapter Seventeen

Anna seized her opportunity, violently pulling on the handle and thrusting the door open. With an unrelenting will, she hurled herself out of the moving vehicle and crashed onto the icy ground with a jarring thud. She tumbled through the snow, her already battered and bruised body absorbing the impact. But despite the pain, she knew this was her chance for escape. She scrambled to her feet and took off, running towards the looming steel beams of the bridge, breathless and desperate to stay alive.

The frigid air clawed at Anna's lungs as she gasped for breath, each icy inhalation a sharp reminder of her life or death situation. Her heart thundered in her chest, a striking difference from the quiet hush of the snow-covered landscape that now served as her escape route. The fine powder beneath her feet seemed to glitter maliciously under the cold silvery moonlight that shone between the rolling clouds, taunting her lack of preparation — no coat to shield her from the biting chill, no shoes to protect her feet from the numbing snow.

Anna could feel the cold seeping through her thinly clad body like a malevolent ghost, gnawing at her flesh with invisible teeth. Her bare feet were rapidly losing sensation, yet she welcomed the numbness, for it lessened the sharp sting of a thousand frozen needles with each desperate step she took. The snow clung to her skin, melting and then chilling again until it felt as if she were running on shards of glass.

Each stride was an act of sheer willpower. With the adrenaline coursing through her veins and the terror propelling her forward, Anna barely noticed how the icy crystals clung to her lashes or how her breath formed frantic puffs of mist that briefly hung in the air before disappearing into the night. She was aware only of the persistent ache in her limbs.

She could see headlights in the distance behind her, signaling help was on its way. But John had abandoned the truck, sprinting towards her with blood dripping from his wounded hand as he aimed the gun at her. "I don't want to shoot you, Anna."

The frigid air clawed at her lungs, aching and burning. Her ribs felt like they were being crushed by an iron vise. But she refused to surrender. She pushed through the biting cold, fighting for every inch of ground. Just as she thought she might make it, his fingers snaked into her hair from behind, yanking her back like a wild animal on a leash.

Despite the searing agony in her scalp, she held back her cries. He twisted her around, his face inches from hers as he taunted, "You belong to me now."

"Let her go," a gruff voice growled. Dwight's form emerged from the dark, his boots softly pounding against the snow-covered road as he moved towards them. He was here! Dwight was here! Her heart leaped in her chest, but the danger loomed close.

Feeling trapped and desperate, John's grip tightened around her neck as he pressed the cold metal of the gun against her temple. She knew she was his last hope, but fear coursed through her veins as she braced for the worst.

"You're not calling the shots, cowboy!" John yelled.

"Let her go and I'll let you walk away."

John scoffed. "And how far do you think I'll get without her?"

Dwight took a step closer. "Farther than you'll get if you don't."

The snow was coming down hard, but Anna kept her eyes fixed on Dwight, searching for any hint of a plan. Did he have one? Maybe he was just buying time until reinforcements arrived. The tension in the air was thick as the standoff continued. Every step John took towards the railing was mirrored by Dwight, each one calculated and deliberate.

Anna watched it all with a sharp eye, wondering who would make the first move. If there was a plan, she hoped he would reveal it soon. She didn't want to go swimming, and they were running out of bridge.

But then, as if on cue, the distant sound of a siren blared through the thick snow. It caught John's attention, giving Dwight the perfect opportunity to relay the secret signal to Anna. He jerked his eyes right. She blinked twice, telling him she'd follow his lead.

Without hesitation, Dwight shifted his gun downwards and squeezed the trigger, sending a bullet straight into John's kneecap. Anna reacted quickly and dove to the right as he'd instructed. But before she could even process what was happening, Dwight was already on top of John, sending them both tumbling over the edge of the railing.

"No!" Anna screamed as she scrambled to her feet, only to see John disappearing into the frigid water below, leaving Dwight hanging onto the lower portion of the bridge.

As she reached him, his eyes met hers. They were a clear, piercing blue, like the heart of a glacier, calm in a way that sent a shiver down her spine—not from the cold, but from the profound tranquility within them. He dangled precariously, one-handed, his other hand outstretched not to her but towards the sky as if bidding farewell to the world he knew he was about to leave.

In that gaze, there was no panic, no fear—just a serene acceptance of his fate. It struck Anna like a physical blow, and for a moment she couldn't breathe. The knowledge that this man who had trained her, protected her, might be moments away from death was inconceivable. Yet here it was—etched into every line of his face—a silent goodbye.

He looked up at her, a smile on his face. "I love you, Anna," he said, his hand slipping from its hold. "No matter what happens, I need you to know that."

Why was he talking like a madman? He was talking about love at a time like this?

"I love you too," she said, thinking he must have hit his head as he went over the edge. She stretched her hand out but couldn't reach him. "But can we talk about this later?"

"No. I should have told you the night we made love, but I was so scared."

"Hold on, Dwight," she said, hoisting her leg over the side and balancing on the narrow beam below.

"Stay where you are!" he told her, a look of terror replacing the grin. "Don't come any closer."

Anna didn't listen. She wouldn't just stand there and watch him die. She knelt, the frigid wind whipping against her cheeks. The metallic chill of the railing dug into her hands as she held on for dear life.

The wind howled around them, biting and unforgiving as it whipped Dwight's hair around his face. The bridge seemed to sway with the force of nature's lament—a mournful dirge for the living soul that hung in the balance.

Anna's lungs refusing to expand as she witnessed the cold, merciless spray of the water below, eagerly reaching up for Dwight like the fingers of death itself.

"Anna, don't," he pleaded. "Please."

"No way, cowboy," she said without hesitation as she reached out and took hold of his wrist. "I'm never letting you go." She looked into his eyes and felt all the love in the world. "Do you hear me? Never."

"You're not strong enough to pull me up, honey."

Anna's heart was beating so fast, a cocktail of desperation and anger brewing inside her. The man before her was surrendering to an end she couldn't accept. "Yes, I am," she said, though she knew he was right. "Now, shut up and let me save you."

Anna's ribs hurt, so much so, that she thought she might vomit. Her muscles screamed in protest. The tendons in her arms stretched taut as steel cables under the strain of Dwight's weight. She could feel his pulse under her fingertips, racing with his exertion and fear. She wished she could pull him up by sheer willpower alone. But she couldn't. "If you go, I go."

With each passing second, the burning in her arms intensified, the pain mingling with a panic that threatened to consume her. Despite the cold, her palms were slick with sweat, betraying her with their slippery grip on Dwight's wrist.

Her breath came in sharp gasps, each one a silent prayer to hold on just a moment longer. She had never known fear like this, a tangible thing that clawed at her insides and screamed at her to hold on until help arrived. But even louder was the determination that resonated through her core, fueled by the steadfast gaze of the man whose life hung quite literally in her hands.

Dwight's eyes were a stormy blue, dark with concern and something else, something that made her heart clench even as it threatened to stop altogether. Love. It was raw and unguarded, laid bare in this moment of peril.

If she was going to die, she wanted to do so looking into the eyes of the man who loved her.

But then a miracle happened.

"No one's going anywhere." In that fleeting moment between despair and surrender came a voice from the snowy darkness.

Anna looked up and into the eyes of the most unlikely savior. "Brian?"

He answered her with a wink. Being a good foot taller than Anna gave him the extra length he needed to grab hold of Dwight's hand. His broad shoulders were tense under his thick rancher's coat. As his fingers closed around Dwight's hand—strong and sure—even the biting chill of the air seemed to hold its breath. With a grunt that mingled with the whistle of the wind, he pulled upward.

The relief was overwhelming as tears streamed down Anna's face. She collapsed on top of Dwight, his strong arms enveloping her as they both caught their breath. Through gasps, he managed to choke out, "Thanks, Brian."

Brian wearily pulled himself to his feet and held out a hand for Dwight to take. "I'm tired of hating you, Dwight," he said, his voice rough with exhaustion.

With an arm around her waist, Dwight accepted the man's hand. As they stood together, she felt a rush of emotions, her heart pounding and tears welling up in her eyes. She didn't want to let go, not now or ever.

As their hands dropped, a charged silence enveloped the air around Dwight and Brian. They were two rugged, rough cowboys, their hearts shattered by the loss of a woman they both loved. Once friends, their grief had driven them apart, creating an insurmountable divide between them.

"You'll never know how sorry I am that I didn't answer that call." Dwight bowed his head, tears welling in his eyes. "That I didn't save her."

Holding back tears of his own, Brian nodded. "It was an accident. No one is to blame."

Anna had never witnessed such a touching moment of love, loss, and forgiveness. She wrapped her arms around Dwight's neck and held on tight. "I love you, Dwight."

He pulled her closer. "I love you too, sweetheart."

The sheriff arrived seconds later, leading a hoard of FBI agents and other first responders.

"We sure know how to draw a crowd, don't we?" she asked, giggling as a deputy hurried to wrap a blanket around her shoulders.

"We sure do," Dwight said, whisking her into his arms.

All was right in Anna's world. She had the man she loved, a family, and a new home.

As the days trickled by, John's lifeless body was found floating in the water miles downstream from where he'd fallen in. Anna was finally cleared of suspicion in his murder, and with Dwight by her side, she gave her official statement about the events leading to Hogue's death.

She recounted to Nolan how Malachi had followed them to a secluded rest stop just over the border into

Montana, brandishing a weapon and demanding the memory card. She revealed how she fought for their lives to wrench the gun from his grasp, and during the struggle, accidentally shot Hogue.

Sharing that had lifted a tremendous burden from Anna's shoulders and gave her peace. In a small gathering of family and friends, she knelt in the calm little meadow just below the ranch house that he had cherished so much.

She opened the urn with shaking hands, watching the weight of the ashes as they slipped to the ground like grains of sand. The gentle breeze carried them away, scattering them over the vibrant spring green grass and newly budding wildflowers.

Tears streamed down her face as she said her final goodbye to Hogue, feeling his presence in every gust of wind and the rustle of leaves around her. It was a peaceful and bittersweet moment, honoring the man who had meant so much to her.

Blake's voice was warm and understanding as she explained to him over the phone and by speaker that she would no longer be taking on the Teton assignment. Because in a few months she'd be too pregnant to do any climbing.

The room had erupted in joyous exclamations, with Lael jumping up and down and shouting with excitement while Dwight was moved to tears, expressing his hope that the baby would be a girl.

Soon after, he'd proposed. It had all been romantic and touching, just the way Anna had always envisioned a proposal should be. They were married in a small ceremony, attended by family and close friends.

Anna stood there, swathed in a dress of delicate ivory lace, feeling as if she were living in a dream. One of the rustic barns had been festooned with twinkling lights and sunflowers, their bright faces turned towards the happy couple like well-wishers. Her bouquet was a wild assembly of daisies, baby's breath, and more sunflowers, tied loosely with a satin ribbon the color of warm honey.

As she had walked down the aisle, every step on the weathered wood floorboards felt deliberate—like the ticking hands of destiny. Brian's eyes had shone with unshed tears that glimmered in the soft light filtering through the barn's aged planks. His large hand had been gentle yet tremulous as he placed it over hers, conveying a silent conversation of pride and affection.

The air was redolent with the mingling scents of fresh hay and blooming flowers. It was as if nature itself conspired to bottle the essence of their love, so potent that Anna could almost taste it on her tongue — sweet as summer lemonade.

Their vows were whispers against the backdrop of quiet sobbing from family members too touched by the scene that unfolded before them.

Life within the walls of the house had also undergone a transformation. Dwight, determined to make a new space for his growing family, had enlisted the help of a contractor to construct an additional bedroom, bath, and adjoining nursery.

The sounds of saws and hammers filled the air as the workers diligently crafted the new space. Meanwhile, Dwight had taken on the task of redecorating the bedroom he'd once shared with Tamara, now transformed into a spacious playroom for Liam and the baby.

Every trace of his late wife had been carefully packed away, save for a few cherished photographs that adorned the walls. But even in her absence, she lingered like a comforting presence, forever etched in the hearts and minds of those who had loved her so fiercely. Her spirit lived on within the walls of their home, a constant re-minder of the love and happiness she had brought into their lives.

Anna wouldn't have wanted it any other way, and she couldn't imagine a more fitting tribute. Her heart felt full and content, as if it had finally found its true direction after being lost for so long.

The memory of that fateful night when Dwight rescued her still brought tears to her eyes, but they were now tears of gratitude and joy. She had been on the wrong path before, but now she was where she was meant to be.

Everything around her seemed to glow with a warm light, as if the universe were smiling down on her and acknowledging her newfound happiness.

Epilogue

Dwight.

Hmm?

Are you awake?

Was he?

He shifted his gaze towards Anna, who lay sleeping next to him. His eyes traced the contours of her face, softened in slumber. The gentle curve of her dark lashes created crescent shadows on her cheeks.

The voice clearly wasn't hers. "I think I am."

His gaze swept the bedroom. No one was there.

Don't be alarmed. It's only me.

He could hardly believe it was her. He hadn't heard her voice in nearly a year. "Tamara?"

Anna stirred beneath the covers.

Shhh... don't wake her. She needs her rest.

He shifted his head on the pillow, not knowing what to say to the voice that he'd once longed to hear.

You don't have to talk. Just listen.

Dwight was confused. Having let go of all the grief and guilt he'd had over Tamara's death, he couldn't understand why she was here now, invading his sleep.

Oh, I think you do.

Did he?

You're worried you won't be there for them.

His chest clamped tight as placed his hand on the gentle swell of Anna's belly, feeling the warmth seeping through the fabric of her nightgown.

As it had over the last few months, an ever-increasing worry swooped in and threatened to paralyze him. This woman, this child and Liam... were his everything. He'd never really gotten his anxiety under control after Tamara died. He'd kept it buried along with his emotions. But as the baby's due-date approached, it was getting harder and harder to fend off.

Tamara was right. He was worried. How could he ever be sure Anna, Liam, and this precious baby would be safe?

Focus on the love, Dwight. That's the only thing that matters. Dangers will come and go, but you have to live in the here and now.

The baby within moved, as if acknowledging his touch. He felt a stirring in his chest, a wonderful blend of love and awe. It felt surreal, this moment suspended between reality and fantasy, where he could almost hear his child's heartbeat intertwining with Anna's steady pulse.

His throat tightened.

Remember. I'm always here if you need me.

Anna rolled over and snuggled closer to him, sighing contently when she'd found a comfortable spot.

But something tells me you won't. She's a wonderful woman, Dwight. Lover her, cherish her and make a lifetime full of happy memories.

I will.

One more thing.

Yes?

It's time.

What?

It's time!

With a jolt, Dwight's eyes shot open, alert and wide. He blinked and pressed his palms against his damp eyes, surprised to find tears there. It was a first for him, as he had never cried in his sleep before. But the dream had been so touching.

The moonlight filtered through the curtains, casting shadows across the room. He heard the sudden rustling on the bed and looked over to see Anna sitting on the edge of the bed, her hands gripping the mattress tightly.

He shot up, adrenaline coursing through his veins as he ran around the bed to where she was. Crouching down in front of her, he searched her face anxiously. "Honey, are you alright?"

She winced and closed her eyes tightly, a moment of agony crossing her features before she looked down at the small puddle forming at her feet. "My water broke," she gasped. "The baby is coming."

Dwight's heart leapt into his throat. He stood up quickly, running his fingers through his hair in disbelief. They were about to have a baby. "Oh, God!" he exclaimed. "Lael!

In a matter of seconds, Lael burst into the room, her eyes bright with excitement and joy.

"Her water broke," he said, pointing to the puddle.

"This ain't your first rodeo, Dwight," she scolded, then chuckled as she helped Anna to her feet. "Don't get your boxers in a bunch."

"He doesn't wear boxers," Anna said, joking through the pain. "He's a brief man."

He couldn't help but think of Lael as his mother-in-law, a title that brought with it a sense of familiarity and acceptance. But in that moment, as he listened to his wife discussing something as personal as his underwear with her, he couldn't help but feel a twinge of discomfort. It was an odd conversation to be having at any time, let alone during such an emotional moment such as this.

But he'd learned that the women in his life, both living and deceased, didn't really give two hoots about his discomfort.

Having helped Anna into a clean gown, Lael cut him a side glance. "You going to the hospital dressed like that?"

Dwight looked down, realizing he was still in his pajama bottoms. "No."

"Then get your clothes on and act like you know what you're doing," she instructed.

"I do know what I'm doing," he defended, feeling the tension ease from his body, leaving the excitement of an expectant daddy in its place.

He dressed in the speed and efficiency of a firefighter suiting up to battle a blazing inferno and started for the stairs.

Don't forget the maternity bag.

"Damn," he swore. "The bag." He spun around and stopped.

Tamara. The dream. A wave of warmth and understanding surrounded him.

Dwight finally got it. All those nights he'd spent raging against the universe, trying to make sense of why his wife was taken from him. He knew now that there was no rhyme or reason to Tamara's death, just cruel fate. Life wasn't fair, and accidents happened.

Things went wrong and when a rancher lost a calf in the dead of a Montana winter, he went looking for it. He didn't stop to answer a phone call.

There were only a handful of things a man could really control and as a husband and father, he'd do everything in his power to keep his family safe. But if he got too caught up in dwelling on the past or even the future, he knew he'd miss so many good things. He had to live in the now and be present. All he had was this moment and Dwight wasn't going to let it slip away.

"My sweet, sweet, Tamara," he whispered. "Thank you."

He reached into the closet and picked up Anna's bag, his heart overflowing with love and hope for the future that lay ahead.

Taking hold of the doorknob, he walked out of the newly built bedroom he shared with Anna and closed the door behind him. "Goodbye, Tamara."

Goodbye, Dwight.

THE END

* 9 7 8 1 7 3 7 5 1 2 7 7 6 *